Dangerous Game

Barbara Spencer

Matador
9 Priory Business Park
Kibworth Beauchamp
Leicestershire LE8 0RX, UK
Tel: (+44) 116 279 2299
Fax: (+44) 116 279 2277
Email: books@troubador.co.uk
Web: www.troubador.co.uk/matador

ISBN 978 1784622 671

British Library Cataloguing in Publication Data.
A catalogue record for this book is available from the British Library.

Typeset in 12pt Garamond by Troubador Publishing Ltd
Printed and bound in the UK by TJ International, Padstow, Cornwall

ALSO BY BARBARA SPENCER

For Children

A Serious Case of Chicken-itis
Scruffy
A Fishy Tail
The Jack Burnside Adventures: A Dangerous Game,
The Bird Children, The Lions of Trafalgar (due 2015).
Legend of the Five Javean
The Amazing Brain of O C Longbotham

For Teens

Time Breaking
Running
Turning Point

Aimee Hilliard 2008

Prologue

All is Lost

The camel, its flanks heaving with exhaustion, trotted on to the high plateau, the long race at breakneck speed over sand and rock finally at an end. Helplessly its rider peered out across the plain towards the high walls of the palace, clearly visible against the setting sun. His hands were clenched into a knot of anger as sounds of battle wafted towards him on the evening breeze, and fear, like a black cloud, drifted high into the sky.

Below him on the pass lay bodies. Men who had lost their lives protecting the narrow way through the mountains to the plain below – slain by treachery. He knew, without looking, that within the palace walls the same scene was being played out. He was too late, he had failed. The palace was gone and with it the only friends he had in the world.

The sun vanished over the horizon, allowing the calm darkness of the night sky to cover the evil before them.

'Arise beast,' he called softly in Arabic and – within seconds – the shadowy outline of a camel stood beside him. Silently, it watched as the fires of battle burned themselves out. Then it spoke.

'The Gods have deserted us, master. Evil has won the day.'

The rider raised his eyes to the sky; deep-set eyes, hidden away from view under the hood of his cloak, eyes which burned with light. He looked far into the distance, as if he were seeing through the darkness into another world.

'There is nothing to be done for now, beast. But one day a boy will come and then we shall see.'

Chapter One

The Last Game of the Season

'Well saved,' the spectators roared as the keeper, diving full length on the ground, scooped the ball from the turf inches from the striker's toes. *'Come on* – get it away.'

'What are you waiting for, Andy?' bellowed Jack, halfway down the pitch. 'Send it down.'

Jack checked the clock, ominously showing two minutes to the final whistle, all the time dancing impatiently from foot to foot.

It had been a tough match, with the other side pushing right from the word go and, at least three times, only the light feet of Andy in goal had kept the ball out of the net. Now, with only two minutes to go, the score remained a tantalising nil-nil.

'We can do it,' Jack called over his shoulder to Saleem, hovering anxiously in left midfield, his words lost in a roar from the watching parents as Andy cleared the ball over the head of the players, straight to Jack's feet.

Now, Jack didn't need to look for Saleem – he knew where he was – because if one of them had the ball the other kept the opposition busy. All Jack had to do was find an opening and his team mate would be waiting.

Jack slid the ball through the first of the bodies blocking him, every eye in the crowd anxiously fixed on the referee, who had pulled out his stopwatch and was officiously studying it. At the same moment Saleem mischievously wrong-footed the two defenders guarding him and, like a vanishing act, reappeared five yards from the post, the defenders hurtling towards the goal to deflect the expected shot.

3

Taking a deep breath Jack left-kicked the ball towards the goal. The shot looked wild, too wild to reach the keeper, and the crowd groaned and clasped their heads in despair. Then Saleem's head collided neatly with the spinning ball, nodding it gently over the heads of the opposition and over the line; the keeper, his hands on his hips, watching in disbelief.

Jack leapt into the air – fist first – as the whistle sounded. Four back flips later Saleem arrived by his side.

'Told you we'd beat'em, Jack.'

Jack laughed. 'And we've only gone and won the trophy, eh Barney?'

Peter Barnabus, the coach in charge of the juniors who trained at the Aston Villa ground, rushed up to his jubilant team scowling horribly.

'Damn nearly lost it rather,' he grumbled. 'Don't leave it so late next time, you two.'

'Oh, I knew we'd win,' said Jack.

'I dunno, whiz kids that's what you are, the whole flippin' lot of you. Good job it's the last game of the season. With luck, your heads'll be back to normal size by September.'

Barney grinned, patting his team of under 13's affectionately on the back. 'Now off you go and get your prize. And don't forget to say thank you.'

The two teams made their way towards the stand, where the mayor was waiting to present the silver trophy, parents and supporters already jostling for the best view. Thirty minutes later it was all over; speeches made and the cup presented. Even photographers from the local newspaper had finished snapping the victorious team, fixed smiles plastered on their faces.

'OK – scram you lot and get showered. I want to go home and put my feet up, even if you don't,' Barney growled, herding the little group of boys into the changing rooms.

After a short while he stuck his head round the locker room door again. 'It's a damn good job you lot don't play at the same speed you shower,' he said. 'At this rate summer training will have begun before you even get home. Move it, can't you.'

Jack bent down to tie his laces, a broad grin on his face. He'd heard it all before. Still Barney had a point. He nudged Saleem, who was changing next to him.

'I'm going down the road before I go home. You coming?'

Saleem nodded, hastily stuffing his wet towel into his bag.

'Pass the word to Andy and Rob. Tell them to hurry, otherwise there'll be a queue.'

A trickle of exhausted spectators, nursing sore hands from clapping too much and hoarse throats from shouting, were still making their way towards the gate as the four boys tore out of the locker room. They pelted down the street towards the nearby chippy, where a queue of hungry people were already impatiently waiting to be served, shouts of 'well done lads' following the boys.

Clutching their trophies of fish and chips, the four friends perched on the kerb with their feet in the gutter. A mouth-watering scent of frying chips and vinegar wafted gently over them.

'Good match,' muttered Rob, chewing thoughtfully.

There was a second or two of silence; his mates, starving after such a momentous game, too busy eating to reply.

By co-incidence they sat in height order. Jack, the tallest, with cropped fair hair, resembled a dyed hedgehog; while Rob, who played central defence, was dark skinned and built more like a rugby player. Next to him sat Andy, the hero of the hour, who was fair with bright red cheeks. The two friends were actually the exact same height although Andy, much to his disgust, looked shorter because of his rotund shape. Last of all came Saleem, the smallest of the quartet, fast and very light on his feet, a lock of jet-black hair constantly tumbling down over his eyes.

'Awesome save, Andy. Thought they'd got it for a moment,' said Jack. 'Barney's bound to give you *man of the match.*'

'But how do you stay so calm?' asked Saleem, chasing a piece of fish round his white polystyrene tray. 'I'd hate it in goal. All those people on the sidelines yelling when you make a mistake. That's scary.'

Andy grinned. 'Yeah, but you can run.' He glanced down at his belly which was swelling rapidly as he downed his chips. 'Anyway goal's easy. It doesn't take a genius to guess which way the ball's coming – watch their eyes.'

'Right, I'm going home.' Rob got to his feet. He screwed his chip tray and paper into a neat package and tossed it into the nearby rubbish bin. 'Mum'll kill me if I'm late. See you next term.'

'I'm going home, too,' said Saleem. He finished the last of his chips and licked his fingers.

'Birming'um home?' asked Jack. Picking up his rubbish he half-turned and lobbed it underarm into the centre of the bin. 'Goal,' he muttered to himself.

'No home, home.'

'Where's that?' said Rob.

'Sudana.'

'*Where's* that?' chimed in Andy.

'Oh! Somewhere over there,' said Saleem waving his hand vaguely in the air.

'Well, where then?' demanded Rob.

'Um! Somewhere in the Sudan?' said Saleem looking slightly uncomfortable.

'*Where's that?*' shouted Rob and Andy together.

'Somewhere in Africa,' laughed Saleem, suddenly figuring out the game his mates were playing.

'*Where's that?*' bellowed Jack joining in the fun, the three boys creating so much noise customers at the tail end of the fish and chip queue turned round to stare.

'Somewhere in the world,' whispered Saleem.

Knowing what was about to happen, he quickly curled himself up in a ball and plastered his hands over his ears. The words *'where's that'* burst over his head like a shock wave, and a ferocious scuffle erupted with all four boys piling in and hitting out enthusiastically. The little line of customers spun round, tut-tut ting as they watched the boys larking about.

'You're back next season, right?' said Jack when he got his breath back. 'I mean we work so great together.'

'The fab two,' agreed Andy. 'Even Barney calls you that.'

'I'll be back,' said Saleem grinning his head off. 'You can bet on it.'

Chapter Two

The Parcel Covered in Stamps

The doorbell rang. Jack cleaning his football boots in the kitchen heard its chime and paused, brush in hand, hoping his mum or sister would go and open it. The bell sounded again, its tone impatient.

'Bother!' he muttered, dropping his boots on the floor. Suddenly remembering it was Christmas in a few days time, he made a dive for the door.

The postman, beaming happily, his arms full of cards and a large, brown-wrapped parcel, called out as Jack opened the door: 'Parcel for you Mrs Burnside and here's one …'

'Mum!' Jack bellowed upstairs. 'Can I sign … '

'Wait!' Thunderous feet pounding down the stairs materialised into his mother. 'I'll take it,' she said firmly, snatching the parcel away from under Jack's nose, carefully tearing away the customs slip as she did so. 'Christmas presents,' she explained to the astonished postman as she signed the receipt. 'To be opened on Christmas day,' she added, frowning at the eager faces of Jack and Lucy huddled together, trying to peek over her shoulder.

'And there's a parcel for you, if you're Jack?' said the postman weakly, finally managing to finish what he'd been trying to say.

Jack nodded eagerly, his eyes fixed on the white box which appeared to be suffering from a bout of measles. One side was covered in small, but powerfully coloured, stamps with Arabic writing on them, while the other was decorated with red arrows, most of which had been scribbled out and over-written in green letters: '*not*

known at this address', 'please forward to Aston Villa', 'try 137 Greenhill Road'.
Somewhere in the middle written in black ink – and hardly visible –
an address:

Jack Burnside, footballer,
Birmingham, England.

Jack wandered back to the kitchen to finish his boots his mind fixed
on the parcel, wondering who on earth could have sent it.

'Oh rats,' he groaned, catching sight of the time. 'Gotta go,' he
shouted to no one in particular and, leaving the box on the kitchen
table, grabbed his jacket making a beeline for the door.

He trotted down the road, looking back over his shoulder to check
on the progress of the bus, sprinting the last fifty metres as it came
into sight. It stopped in response to his arm, stuck straight out like a
rigid barrier, and he hopped on grinning as he saw his two pals
sprawled across one of the seats.

Jack flashed his bus pass. 'Aston Villa …'

'I know that by now,' rebuked the driver. 'But what surprises me,
is why a great team like Manchester United allow their star player –
Jack Burnside, who incidentally scored twice last night – to ride on a
bus. You'd *think* they could afford a taxi.'

Jack groaned, keeping his face polite, since the driver made the
same joke, with small variations, every single time he saw him – which
was three times a week … every week. And after the first trillion times,
it wasn't funny. It was only funny when his dad said it: 'Have you met
my son, Jack Burnside, the footballer?'

His dad's friends would turn, gazing excitedly, seeing the same
height – tall and lanky – the same colour eyes and the same fair hair,
sheared as short as Jack's mother would allow. And, for a moment or
two, he got away with it, until they realised Jack was too young and
his dad was only pulling their leg.

I'd be a dead ringer too if Mum would only let me wear earrings, like he does, thought Jack indignantly. Still, none of that made the slightest bit of difference – the conductor was still a total loser.

'Anyone heard from Saleem?' he asked, crashing down in the seat behind his pals.

Rob and Andy shook their heads.

'If anyone does, it'll be you,' said Andy. 'Why?'

'Got this weird parcel in the post. How it got to me I haven't a clue, 'cos it didn't have the right address and it's bin everywhere. It doesn't say who it's from though and I wondered if it was Saleem.'

'What's in it?' said Rob.

Jack shrugged. 'Dunno! Didn't open it yet.'

'Can't be Saleem,' said Andy firmly, 'he knows where you live.'

'Odd though,' agreed Rob. 'He goes back to his own country and no one hears from him ever again. S'pose they don't have phones where he comes from.'

Jack shook his head. 'Course they do. Dad's working in the desert and he phones home all the time. I even asked Barney. He said the club hadn't heard a word and they had to let his place go to this new kid, Leonard. So what do you think of him?' he said, changing the subject.

'Who, the Nerd?' said Andy.

'Yeah, the kid with two left feet,' moaned Jack, 'and I had to partner him last week.'

The Aston Villa ground came into sight. Jack jumped up and rang the bell. The bus slowed.

'Bagsy, I don't partner the Nerd then,' shouted Rob, leaping off before the bus had stopped, earning him a ticking off from the driver.

'Hey! That's not fair, I did it last week,' grumbled, Jack catching up with him. 'It freaks me out. He spends all his time bagging the ball, I never get a go, and if he says just one more time: *let me try it again, Jack, I nearly got it that time,* I'll kill him.'

'He doesn't bother me none,' Andy said.

'Because you're in goal, der brain,' moaned Jack. 'Please, Rob, swap.'

'OK! I'll do it next week,' Rob said

Andy nudged him. 'We're not playing next week,' he whispered in Rob's ear. 'It's Christmas, remember.'

'I know,' Rob grinned.

Half-an-hour later Jack had had enough. They'd completed twenty minutes warm-up exercises and were now practising ball skills, except he was standing still while Leonard hogged the ball. Jack glared at his watch, wishing the session was over.

'Please, please, please come back Saleem and save me from dying of boredom,' he muttered, then shouted impatiently: 'Come on, pass the ball, we're supposed to be working together, remember.'

Leonard threw the ball and Jack ran forward to take the pass still thinking about Saleem. It came in wide. Jack scuffed his toe in the dirt and stumbled missing the ball, which trickled sadly off towards the goal.

'What the hell are you doing, Jack, *stargazing?*' Barney bellowed.

Angry with himself, Jack collected the ball and looked across the pitch to see Barney waving his arms impatiently.

'Sorry,' he said.

Barney heaved an angry sigh. 'Try it again. Leonard, send the ball in.'

The boy nodded and, taking the ball from the despondent figure of Jack, trotted back to his place on the pitch. The ball came in again and Jack, knowing Barney was still watching, made sure he did it right. Trapping it with his left shin, he let it drop before dribbling it towards the goal.

'*Yes!*' he whispered to himself, banging his fists at the air. He flashed a quick glance at the side lines hoping he was off the hook.

11

When the whistle blew for the end of the session, the thirty or so boys ran off to shower and change. Some minutes later, the three friends emerged from the locker-room to see Barney busily packing away the practice balls, his head deep inside the big equipment cupboard.

'Jack, a word,' he called over his shoulder.

Jack sauntered over prepared for yet another rollicking.

'What the hell's the matter with you these days, you're all over the place?'

'Sorry, Barney, won't let it happen again.'

Barney took his head out of the cupboard long enough to glare. *'You bet your life, you won't.* You'll never make the under-14 team at this rate, in which case you and I will be having a serious chat about your future with this squad. I used to be able to rely on you, Jack. All of a sudden, you've got two left feet. What's going on? Bored with training?'

'You know I'm not,' said Jack, trying to keep his voice low, aware that Andy and Rob were lingering close by on purpose to listen in.

'So what?'

'Dunno!'

'Well you'd better find out *and quick.* I shall be expecting better things from you next term or else.'

Jack nodded miserably.

Barney turned to the groups of boys wandering out of the locker room. 'Have a good break, lads; see you after Christmas.'

The three friends strolled out of the training ground.

'So what'd'he say?' said Andy.

'Says he's going to drop me unless things get better,' said Jack dramatically, trying to stop himself bursting into tears.

'Nah, he won't do that,' said Rob, punching him on the arm. 'You're too good. My dad says you're just going through a bad patch.

He says no footballer likes playing with someone new.' Rob screwed up his face. 'Except, to be honest, I don't think you'll ever get used to the Nerd.'

'Don't you just know it,' replied Jack. 'Stupid kid doesn't know the meaning of sharing the ball. Then it's me Barney has a go at,' he grumbled.

'Forget it. It's Christmas in a few days. What are you doing?'

'Being bored by relatives. Still, I got a prezi from Dad though, came this morning.'

'What's in it?'

'Dunno. Mum's hidden it.'

'Cheer up.' Andy clapped him on the back. 'Something exciting will happen; it always does.'

'Don't hold your breath!' said Jack, feeling totally pessimistic. 'Come on, there's a bus coming, let's run.'

* * *

'Good session,' his mother called out as Jack arrived home. He stuck his head round the door and she looked up, pausing in her task of rolling pastry.

'Mum,' he asked. 'Can I open my parcel?'

'No,' she replied. 'It's Christmas, remember? So forget about it and take your bag upstairs.'

'Has Dad phoned today?'

She shook her head. 'Why, is there something wrong?'

Jack flushed. 'No,' he said quickly. 'It's nothing. Just wish I could go there for the holidays that's all,' he muttered. 'Hot sun and ...'

'Sand and mosquitoes,' added his mother, opening the oven door to put in her mince pies, a blast of hot air flooding out into her face. 'Perhaps next year if you're good.'

'But it's going to be really *awful* without him,' Jack burst out suddenly, 'especially if we've got to put up with relatives.'

'Oh, come on, Jack, it won't be that bad. I know Grandma Sideburns ...'

'*Mum!*'

'Hey! You don't think I *know* what you call her?' laughed his mother.

Jack grinned shamefaced.

'*And I know* your Auntie Maeve will spend all her time picking on you, and telling you that football is a waste of time.'

'*And* Cousin Richard will be a right bore, 'cos he'll talk fishing all day,' added Jack.

'Stop worrying, Jack, we'll survive the relative attack. It's sad Dad can't be with us, but he's just too far away. Have a mince pie, that'll cheer you up.'

Jack continued upstairs to his bedroom, clutching a plate with two crisp tartlets bulging with mincemeat. He plonked himself down on the floor beneath his life-size poster of Jack Burnside, the Manchester United and England superstar.

'I bet you never had to play with a nerd,' he grumbled to the footballer. He took a mouthful of mince pie and flicked the switch on his TV, his DVD player whirring into action. He was so engrossed in the action sequences he didn't even hear the phone ringing.

'Jack? Dad wants to talk to you,' his mother shouted from the bottom of the stairs.

He leapt for the stairs, descending two a time, and grabbed the phone.

'Mum says you're having problems at football.'

His dad's voice sounded tinny, a million miles away.

'It wasn't anything,' Jack mumbled, furious that his mother always knew when something went wrong.

'So tell me.'

Jack sighed loudly. 'Well, it's just that football's not been going so well this term.'

'And Peter Barnabus bawled you out, did he?'

Jack mumbled something down the receiver.

'Let me tell you something about Barney,' his dad continued. 'He'll only bawl you out if you're any good, otherwise he doesn't bother. Okay?'

Jack grinned. 'Yep! Thanks, Dad.'

'So what happened?'

'It's this new kid, Leonard, the one who took Saleem's place. We can't work together and it shows. I mean he's never about when I want him, goes it alone and then swears I told him something else.'

'And did you?'

'As if!'

'Sounds tricky, but that doesn't mean you stop trying.'

'I guess I have, Dad,' Jack admitted reluctantly. 'But ...'

'Jack!'

'OK, you're right – no excuses. I'll do better next term, promise.'

'Any other problems?'

'No – except Christmas. It's going to be a real bummer without you – and last year was terrific. We saw Aston Villa v Blackburn on Boxing Day, remember?'

His dad laughed. 'Can't do that, Jack, however much we want to. Aston Villa aren't playing Blackburn on Boxing Day.'

Jack laughed, feeling heaps better. 'Dad, you remember Saleem? When he went back home I gave him your number. Don't suppose he's been in touch, has he?'

'No, why?'

''Cos I never heard from him after he left, and he was my best mate at football.'

'Can't help, sorry. By the way, I told your mother to let you open my present on Christmas Eve. Have fun on your own before Grandma arrives – hissing and spitting fire.'

'Wow, Dad, thanks,' Jack whooped.

'Speak to you on Chr .. . ch … ch … ch …'

And with that, the line went dead.

Chapter Three

The Shadow on the Wall

Christmas Eve was fun, with games and a picnic in front of the television while they watched a movie. As the credits flashed up Jack, unable to stand the suspense any longer, dived under the Christmas tree pulling three packages from the brightly coloured pile.

His was long and flat with something soft inside. Determined to be last to open his present, he waited impatiently while Lucy slowly picked off each strip of selotape, carefully smoothing out the star-covered wrapping paper to use again, and taking such a long time, Jack began to wonder if they'd still be there next Christmas. Inside was a long sparkly dress which Lucy immediately began swishing backwards and forwards, cooing with happiness as the material changed from silver to gold and purple.

'That's fantastic, Luce,' Jack said and ripped through the paper round his present, pulling out the latest Manchester United team football shirt, emblazoned with the magical words, *no 7 – Jack Burnside*. He beamed. 'Wow! Trust Dad to know exactly what I wanted.'

He gazed across at his mother, who was already wearing her gift, a silver necklace carved with palm trees, the expression on his face so like a dog begging for a bone, she began to laugh.

'I suppose you want to open that now?' she said, glancing towards the multi-coloured box sitting under the tree.

He nodded.

'All right, I guess you can. I know you're dying to.'

'Thanks, Mum.'

He tore the wrapping paper from his parcel. Inside was a cardboard box. He pulled it open, using both hands to dive into its depths.

'Hey, that's nice,' said his mother, as he lifted out a statue of a camel. 'Let's have a closer look, Jack. See, it's carved from a single piece of wood. How unusual. So who's it from?'

Jack rummaged in the box, inspecting every shred of paper closely. 'There's no card,' he said, shaking his head. He picked up the box turning it round and round. 'But it's got to be Saleem, I don't know anyone else.'

'I expect he forgot to put the card in.'

Jack nodded. 'Guess so, but it's a real bummer. I can't even say *thank you* 'cos I don't have his address.'

'Come on, Lucy,' Mrs Burnside yawned. 'It's way past your bedtime, yours too, Jack. It's Christmas tomorrow, remember.'

'Why did you have to go and remind me.' Jack got reluctantly to his feet, slowly following his sister up the stairs. 'It's going to be a real drag.'

'At least we had fun tonight, Jack, and it's only one day.'

'I s'pose. Night, Mum.'

Jack opened his bedroom door and, putting on the light, carefully placed his gifts on top of his clothes chest before going into the bathroom to clean his teeth.

'Night, Luce,' he called.

Lucy peered round her bedroom door. 'Do you think Father Christmas will come?'

'Yeah, course. Night.'

'Happy Christmas.'

'Right!' Jack shut his bedroom door and, going over to the chest, picked up the wooden carving studying it closely. It was quite small, only about thirty centimetres high, but extraordinarily life-like. The camel's head was held majestically, the sneer on its face plainly visible. The wood felt warm and velvety and there were light sandy splotches on it, like sand in the desert.

'You can live on my window sill,' he said to the wooden statue, 'where I can keep an eye on you.' He drew back his curtains and peered out but there was nothing to see, only boring blackness without any stars. He pressed his nose against the glass, trying to see as far as the lamppost on the corner of the street.

'Wish I was spending Christmas in the Sudan like Dad,' he grumbled, 'where it's hot and sunny, not here where it's cold and wet with nothing but manky old relatives to look forward to.' The glass was freezing and he rubbed his nose to warm it. 'S'pose I might as well go to bed. Goodnight, Bud,' he said and, patting the wooden camel on its rump, switched off his light and climbed into bed.

Beams of light drifted in from the lamppost lifting the darkness of his room and alighting on the camel, cast its shadow onto the far wall. Jack gazed at the statue for a while, getting sleepier and sleepier as the warmth of his bed closed in around him. The shadow on the wall seemed to stretch, expanding in the light beams, its dark shape swelling until it filled the whole wall. Jack felt his eyelids closing. He burped loudly and fell asleep.

How long he'd been asleep he didn't know, but something woke him. Sleepily he lay and listened.

'Salaam Aleikoum!' a voice said.

The sound came from inside his room. Jack sat up in bed, wide awake, clutching the sheets to his chest.

'Salaam Aleikoum,' the voice came again, the words harsh and uncompromising. Then came a noise rather like a railway engine bursting out of a tunnel and someone spat loudly. '*Pfliipft!*'

Jack ducked, expecting something heavy to come hurtling in his direction. He made a grab for the light, its sudden brightness obliterating all the shadowy corners of his room. Astonished, he gazed round but there was no one there, the room was empty. *So what had made the noise?* Slowly he looked again, inspecting every inch, even ducking down to look under his bed. He checked again frowning, his eyes darting suspiciously from side to side. But nothing had moved or was any different from when he went to bed.

Had he dreamt it? His mother was always saying that overeating gave you nightmares. It was just possible he had eaten too much supper; three mince pies, an ice cream and a bag of crisps might well be considered way too much after a large helping of lasagne.

Jack slowly began to relax, sleepily deciding it might be a good idea to wear his new shirt on Christmas morning to annoy Auntie Maeve. Leaving the light on, he let his head drift back down onto the pillow.

'Can't you switch off the light, infidel,' said the voice.

Jack froze, too scared to move. 'Who's there? Show yourself,' he croaked, sounding as if he had a bad cold.

'Pflüpft!' The noise of spitting came again. 'I said switch off that dam-ned light.'

Trembling, Jack did as he was told. 'Wh ... Wh ... Wh ... Where are you?' he quavered, looking at the blackness around him, his eyes slowly adjusting to the light cast by the street lamp.

'Back wall,' ordered the voice.

Jack turned and looked slowly over towards the wall. On it was the shadow of a camel. Menacing, dominant, it towered over the room. Then the head of the shadow moved, turned, and looked straight at him.

'Salaam Aleikoum!'

Jack jumped violently. 'Sala-ar-m what?' he stuttered.

'Aleikoum! Aleikoum! You pathetically minded individual. It means God go with you. As a form of greeting it is beyond parallel.'

'Beyond what?' Jack said.

'Parallel! Parallel! May god preserve us! Are you witless?'

'No, of course I'm not. It's just that I've never heard anyone say parallel before, except in a maths lesson.'

'In a *what* lesson?'

'A maths lesson! A maths lesson! Are you stupid?' retorted Jack, his courage suddenly blasting back into place.

The camel's head turned away, followed by the spitting noise. '*Pflüpft!*'

'Hey! Don't spit in my room.'

'Camels spit. That's what we do.'

'I know, but *not* in my room.'

'This is getting us nowhere,' said the camel in a resigned tone. 'Why do all conversations with christians end up going nowhere?'

Jack ignored the remark, uncertain how to answer it anyway. 'Who are you?' he said.

'It would appear my name is Bud,' the camel remarked haughtily.

'Bud! But I don't know a ...' Jack gazed at the empty space on the windowsill, where the small statue had stood. 'Oh!' he said and turned round again, a bewildered expression on his face. 'But what are you doing here?'

Bud moved his head. 'I have been sent to fetch you.'

'Sent to fetch me?'

'Why do you repeat everything I say?' The camel glared at the boy, only his head visible above the bedclothes.

''Cos I don't understand what you're saying.'

'Am I not talking in your language; English, I think it is.'

'Yes, you are,' replied Jack irritably, his fear forgotten. 'And I still don't understand. Anyhow, I'm not going anywhere. My mum would kill me if I left the house at this hour.'

A rude noise, rather like a balloon deflating, filled the room and the shadow begin to shrink. It paused muttering, 'But why would a mere female kill her offspring? *Most unlikely.'* Then – as if it had second thoughts – filled out again. 'Did you not, only a minute ago, express the wish to go to the Sudan to bask in the sunshine?' it asked.

'That's different,' replied Jack. Feeling bolder, he pushed back the bedclothes and sat cross-legged facing the shadow. 'It's different wishing to do something and actually *doing* it.'

'And I thought when I found Jack Burnside … by the way *are* you Jack Burnside?' Jack nodded. 'I would find someone brave and daring, ready for great adventures. I see I was wrong,' the camel said with a sneer.

'*That's all you know about it,*' Jack retorted. He paused frowning and asked: 'Anyhow, what sort of adventures? You talking about the Sudan?'

The shadow nodded.

'But how do you get there? I mean, and I don't want to be rude or anything, but camels plod.'

The camel glared offended. 'I do not plod. I fly on a pathway in the sky made from beams of light, which the sun discards in its daily journey from east to west. And it is my master who commands me to take you to the Sudan, from where I will return you before dawn. This will be good, for your mother will remain unaware you have left the house and therefore *will have no need to kill you.*'

Jack jumped. 'Stop shouting,' he whispered. 'You'll wake my mother.'

The camel spat contemptuously. '*Pflüpft!* Magical camels do not wake people unless they intend to do so.'

Jack stared at the wall transfixed, unable to believe what he was actually seeing.

The shadow had removed itself from the surface of the wall, and was now plumping up its sides to become three-dimensional. A moment later it was fully grown, hairy and smelly, and taking up most of the space in his bedroom.

Jack flinched back out of the way. 'Whoa!' he gasped, his courage suddenly melting away like an ice cube. 'Thanks, but no thanks,' he shook his head. *This is way too freaky.'*

There was a silence. Jack, looking up, saw the camel watching him closely, all the time chewing the cud. Then it spat. 'Are you usually this difficult?'

'Yes,' Jack said concealing a grin.

'Then, it is beyond my considerable understanding how a person like Saleem could possibly call you a friend.'

'*Saleem?* What about Saleem?'

'You know him?'

'Of course I know him, he's a mate,' Jack said impatiently. 'What's happened to him?'

'He is in danger and asks his friend, Jack Burnside, to help him.'

Jack jumped straight out of bed. 'Jeez! Why didn't you tell me this straight off? Course I'll come.'

'Amazing!' said the camel.

'You're sure we'll be back before dawn so I won't be missed?'

'Inshallah! Please bedeck yourself in warm clothing and remember to bring your football boots.'

'Why my football boots?' Jack gazed at the camel in surprise.

'Are you not a footballer?'

'Yes, but …'

'Then you are to bring your football clothes and boots.'

Jack opened his mouth to ask a question and hastily shut it again, spotting the glare on the camel's face. Quickly pulling on the clothes he'd been wearing, he grabbed his kit bag and set about filling it, promising to make a determined effort not to eat quite so much in the future, if weird things like this were going to happen. He pushed his football into his bag and, as an afterthought, added his new shirt, laying it right on top. His bag was now full so, tying his boots together, he slung them round his neck. Then, taking a deep breath, climbed carefully on to his bedroom chair and grabbed the harness, his boots rasping against the leather saddle as he pulled himself up.

The camel's coat felt woolly and had a musty smell, as if it had been stored in a damp cupboard. Jack wedged himself against the hump for safety, surprised to find it soft and spongy, since he'd always imagined a camel's hump to be hard, like bone. Timidly he caught at the reins, grasping them tightly as the camel began to move heading for the wall of his bedroom.

The bricks melted away and, to his astonishment, he found himself in the street. 'Wow!' he exclaimed breathlessly.

There was a flash of lightning and stars flew around helter-skelter, like leaves being chased by the wind. Terrified he might fall, Jack clung to the reins shutting his eyes tightly. An icy cold wind began to blow, finding its way into every crevice of his clothing. Great gusts tore at his jacket and jeans trying to unseat him and he wished now he'd put on gloves, his fingers frozen.

After a while, when nothing terrible had happened, he opened first one eye then the other cautiously looking round. But there was nothing to be seen, only the blackness of the night sky, stars shining brightly in the distance.

'So how do you know Saleem?' he said, asking the first of a hundred questions burning away in his brain.

There was no reply.

Jack tried again. 'And why is he in danger?'

'Be silent, infidel.'

'Why,' he said indignantly.

'Even a magical camel, as superior as I, will find it difficult to outrun the sun if using their breath to talk.'

24

'Oh,' said Jack, beginning to feel anxious. 'What happens if you *don't* outrun the sun?'

'I turn back into a block of wood.'

Jack yelped loudly. '*So what happens to me if* **you** *turn into a block of wood?*'

'*You? You* fall out of the sky.'

Chapter Four

The Woodcarver cum Merchant cum Soothsayer

He must have dozed, for when Jack looked about him again the wind had dropped and it was much warmer. He looked down. No wonder; they were on the ground, silently moving between rows of dark, shadowy houses. Even the dense blackness of the English winter had vanished. The darkness now surrounding him was navy blue, the sky lit by millions of stars.

'Have we far to go?' he said.

'We have arrived.'

A stable door opened and they trotted through into a lamp-lit room, the doors closing behind them. A man in striped robes, covering him from head to toe, stood waiting for them. His back was bent and his shoulders hunched, wrapping themselves round his neck, rather like a tall man trying to look shorter. His hands moved continuously, rubbing themselves against one another as if he was washing them. He didn't speak. Instead, he placed his two hands together, fingertips touching, and bowed low towards the camel.

'Yes, we're back,' said Bud belligerently. 'Am I surprised you didn't happen to mention that I was to be sent halfway round the world? Thanks to you, I had to travel fast to reach your miserable hovel before dawn.'

'A-thousand-pardons, curs-ed beast.' The man glanced in Jack's direction and beckoned. 'Climb down, my Lord. Welcome to my humble abode.'

Jack slid to the ground, feeling the camel's back turn to jelly, shrinking and sliding away from him. Curiously, he turned to watch as the flesh and bone of the camel vanished, melting into the wall and leaving just a shadow.

'Where am I?' he asked nervously, looking round the stable.

'You are in the home of Jacob, a sometime woodcarver cum merchant cum soothsayer.' It was the camel's voice.

Jack stared at the wall, where the shadow of the camel loomed. 'Jeez! You gave me a fright. You can still talk?'

'But of course! Surely your brain is capable of remembering, that it was from a shadow on the wall that I first addressed you.'

'Er ... what! Oh yes, I forgot.'

'As long as this room is dark and lit only by a lamp, remember that, you curs-ed beast. I have only to open the windows and let the sun in,' said Jacob. He spoke humbly, as if the world was doing him a big favour by allowing him to speak at all. 'It is good to meet you, my Lord Burnside,' he said turning towards Jack. 'Please accept my most heartfelt thanks for your kind offer of help. There is food, look.' He stretched out his arm towards the table. 'Eat! Eat! You will be weary from your journey.'

'I know I am only a beast of burden, who is of little or no consequence,' interrupted the shadow. 'But I'd also like some fodder, if there is some going. Fresh hay made from date palms would be my preferred choice but, of course, I would eat anything you consider offering me, oh accurs-ed one.'

Jacob threw a small bale of hay at the shadow on the wall. To Jack's astonishment the pale brown nose of the camel projected itself out of the wall and started munching.

Jack sat down at the table. What had Andy said about something exciting turning up? Well it had and it was dead freaky, except for the food which looked fantastic.

'Please can you tell me what's happened to Saleem? *Mmm! This is great*, what is it?' he mumbled, his mouth full.

'Camel stew, my Lord,' replied the merchant, glaring at the munching nose.

The shadow glared back and spat loudly.

'Allow me to make amends for this ignorant beast who, by rights, should be as extinct as the Dodo.' Jacob's tone changed, becoming as smooth as velvet. 'Eat first, my Lord Burnside. I will explain everything before we go to the palace.'

'*Palace!* What palace?'

'The palace where your friend, Saleem, is imprisoned.'

'*Imprisoned!*' Jack swung round to stare at the merchant, who was standing at his elbow, his hands circling round one another like a guinea pig on a running wheel. 'You've gotta be joking.'

Jacob shook his head. 'The palace I speak of is in the Kingdom of Sudana, a small but peaceful land, many miles from here. Alas, it is no longer peaceful, for a Prince Saladin now rules the kingdom. He is a usurper, for whom the throne was never intended. Nevertheless, he is the incumbent and therefore ruler of its people. And, indeed, not only Saleem has disappeared, everything I hold dear has vanished, including my jewelled box.'

'Don't forget your daughter,' reminded the camel.

'I meant my daughter.' The merchant glared at the shadow on the wall, while his hands dived into the voluminous sleeves of his robe and disappeared. 'Mercedes, the light of my life.'

'So it wasn't Saleem that sent the camel – it was you,' Jack guessed.

Jacob inclined his head. 'Naturally. I have sought hard and long for ways to enter the kingdom to find them, for no one is allowed in or out, without the permission of the prince,' he said.

'So how do I come into it?' Jack interrupted with a puzzled frown.

Jacob's arms soared into the air, as if practising semaphore. *'But that is what I am telling you, my Lord!* I learned that the Prince Saladin has a passion for the game of football,' he added more calmly, 'and desired a coach for his team. I remembered young Saleem speaking about his friend – Jack Burnside – with whom he played football. I know nothing of the game, but even I have heard of the famous English footballer and have seen the red football shirts hanging in the market place, with his name on them.

'It was then I had this most brilliant idea,' he continued. 'If I could give the Prince Saladin what he desired, a coach for his football team, surely not even he would suspect that such a man could be a spy. That is why I sent the beast to find you. Once inside the palace you can search at night and coach the team by day. Indeed, when I told the Prince that a famous footballer was to visit him – and not only a famous footballer but *the most famous of footballers* – he was most delighted.'

'What's that!' exclaimed Jack, dropping his fork in astonishment.

'Which piece of my most miserable history did you not understand, my Lord?'

'The famous footballer bit, I think,' Jack said cautiously.

'Why, that is you, my Lord! And it is indeed a most brilliant idea, for I knew Saleem's friend would be only too happy to help us. And, as you see,' Jacob bowed low towards Jack, 'you have come.'

'But *I'm* not Jack Burnside!'

'My Lord jests!'

'*Stop calling me, my Lord.* My name's Jack Burnside all right, but I'm not the Jack Burnside you want. *I'm Jack Burnside, a schoolboy from Birmingham.*'

'*But you have the boots.*' Jacob's voice ascended like the siren of a ship into a banshee wail.

'Yes,' agreed Jack, '*and* sometimes I support Manchester United but *I'm* not *Jack Burnside.*'

'*Why, for what reason, are you not Jack Burnside?*'

'For one thing I'm only thirteen and he's nearly twenty.'

'Ooops!' The camel's nose stopped munching hay and withdrew into the safety of the wall.

'I rain curses on you, you curs-ed mongrel.' Jacob glared at the camel. 'Oh Jehovah rid me of this curs-ed monstrosity of a carbuncle, who brings me a look-a-like of the real thing,' he shouted, wringing his hands, throwing his fist at the ceiling and a pot at the wall.

'Now, don't you go blaming me, old man, I didn't hatch this plan. And, don't you go forgetting it was *you* who sent me to fetch the footballer.'

'But you didn't fetch the footballer, did you – *you four-legged albatross of the Sahara,*' shouted the merchant, flinging his arms into the air in supplication.

Insults were now flying round the room, the camel getting in as many hits as his master, forcing Jack to suspend eating and stop up his ears, which were ringing with a quantity of Arabic curses.

'*Hello-o? Anybody there?*' he shouted over the noise.

Silence.

'A-thousand-pardons. I shall let the sun in directly so you need not suffer the vulgarity of this beast, my Lord.'

'I don't advise it, you sour-faced old man. You still need me to take the boy back and find the real Jack Burnside.'

'You know where he lives then?' Jack eyed the camel, a broad grin on his face.

'No, but England is a small country, I would soon find him.' The camel looked down his nose at the boy and leered.

'I don't *think* so,' said Jack, sounding smug. 'There are at least sixty million people in England; he won't be that easy to find.'

He turned round to stare at the merchant, who was wandering round and round in circles, his arms thrust high into the air, his fingers outstretched as if he was carrying a heavy boulder.

'Isn't there another way?' Jack said.

Never ceasing his pacing, the merchant muttered, 'I have tried all other ways.'

'Oh!' Jack shrugged. 'Sorry, I'd like to have helped,' he said, undecided whether he was relieved to be going home or disappointed he couldn't help Saleem.

The merchant stopped his wandering and looked fixedly at Jack from under his eyebrows, burying his hands in the front of his robe to stop their incessant movement.

'Maybe you can, my Lord.'

'How?' Jack said startled, quickly adding, 'I'm not Jack Burnside, remember.'

'But you play football?'

'Y-yes!' agreed Jack cautiously, wondering what was coming.

'I could make it so that you look like Jack Burnside.'

'I *do* look like Jack Burnside,' protested Jack indignantly, 'except I look younger than him.'

'Nevertheless, I can bind the Prince's eyes – and those of every man who serves him. When they look at you, they will see only what I wish them to see.'

'Can he really do that?' Jack turned to the camel.

The shadow nodded soberly, stretching its neck out of the wall to pick up another mouthful of hay from the bundle.

'The accurs-ed one can be very tricky. You need to have eyes in the back of your head when he's about.'

'But I could never pass as the real thing,' Jack admitted reluctantly.

'Look in this mirror, my Lord.'

In a corner of the room stood a long mirror. Jack hadn't noticed it before but then, if he were honest, he'd been too busy eating to notice anything much. He got slowly to his feet peering round the shadowy space. In one corner, bales of hay had been stacked like the one Bud was chewing at. On the opposite side of the room, between two wooden uprights, someone had strung a curtain, its stripes matching those of Jacob's robe. Behind it, Jack caught a glimpse of a bed and a pile of wooden plates and cooking utensils lying on a shelf. So this room was actually Jacob's house.

He stared at his reflection in the mirror, watching curiously as his silhouette began to alter, the muscles becoming more defined, his face putting on years. A moment later there, gazing back at him, was a genuine look-a-like of the great man. Jack waved feebly at the footballer who waved back, his mouth – like Jack's – falling open in astonishment.

'Is ... that ... really ... what they'll see?'

The merchant nodded.

'Jeez!' Jack hurriedly sat down again, in case his legs gave way. He was silent for a moment. 'If that's all there is to it ...' he began.

The shadow stopped chewing, its eye fixed on Jack.

Jacob nodded encouragingly. 'Yes, yes?'

'Then I s'pose it's possible for me to do what you want,' he finished the sentence.

There was a sharp exhalation of breath from the wall.

'So what is it you want me to do, again?' Jack frowned, 'train a football team to play a match while I'm searching for Saleem? I've helped out with the kids at school heaps of times, so how hard can that be. Oh ...' his face fell. 'Sorry, that can't work either. I've got to be back by morning; Bud promised.'

'I never promise,' said the shadow haughtily.

Jack spun round glaring at the wall. 'Yes, *you did, you promised*,' he insisted.

'I lied,' said Bud. 'Well, actually I didn't lie. I said *Inshallah*, which means if God wills. Obviously God doesn't will it.'

'*That's it!*' shouted Jack angrily. '*Take me home, right now!*'

'*Hss! Hss!*' The merchant waggled his arms in the air, like someone with bubble gum stuck to his fingers. 'There is time. The match takes place on the twenty-fourth day of the last month of the year.'

'But that's Christmas Eve!'

'What is this Christmas, my Lord?'

'It's a big holiday,' said Jack eagerly. 'We give presents and have lots to eat and good TV, and all our relatives come to call.'

'That is not a good thing, this seeing of the relatives. *That* is not a holiday, *that is simply a most painful duty*,' said the merchant seriously.

Jack grinned. 'Especially if you have some like mine. Hang on! If the match is on the twenty-fourth, it's happened already.'

Jacob shook his head. 'No, my Lord, the twenty-fourth is still seven moons away.'

'Moons?' Jack repeated cautiously, pronouncing the word as if it might jump up and bite him.

'Each moon is but one whole day, my Lord.'

Jack stared at Jacob, his mouth dropping open. 'You mean it's seven days away! A week? It can't be … can it?'

Jacob nodded.

'But how? I mean … I mean … *how*?'

'This land they call the Sudan is so vast that much time can be wasted travelling across it,' Jacob said somewhat obscurely.

Jack stared at him blankly. 'So you mean that *here*,' he emphasised the word, 'time is different?'

'No! No! No!' Jacob waved his arms vigorously, as if the continent of Africa was an eel that he was trying to stuff into a small box. 'Time here is the same as in the outside world.' He stopped and thought for a moment. 'Perhaps a little slower,' he admitted, 'since we do not have television. It was your journey with that curs-ed beast that altered the time.'

Jack frowned, trying to figure out how he could have spent the entire night travelling east, only to find himself arriving at his destination seven days before he set out. He stared at the shadow on the wall, its pale brown nose busily continuing to munch at the bale of hay. Still, it wasn't exactly usual to come across a camel that could fly. Or one, he hastily corrected himself, that started the day as a wooden ornament. On the other hand, he could still be dreaming, in which case it didn't much matter about time getting out of sync because any moment now he'd wake up.

'And I'm really not dreaming?'

'No, my Lord Burnside.'

'Wicked! So that means …' Jack said, working it out. He thought for a moment calculating. *If Christmas Eve is still seven days away…* He finished the sentence aloud. 'That means I can help you and still get home.'

'Yes, my Lord, so it does. Have some sweets,' said the merchant pushing a plate across the table.

'Okay, in a minute,' Jack replied, still thinking it through. Absentmindedly he picked up one of the small cakes glistening with honey. 'And would Bud take me?' he muttered, taking a large bite. The cake burst open and rivulets of honey dribbled down his chin, his tongue chasing them. He licked his lips eyeing the plate greedily.

'No, my Lord, I will take you to the palace and present you to its ruler. That curs-ed ship of the desert, whom you seem content to call Bud, will travel in your bag,' Jacob pointed to the rucksack on the floor. 'Then, when darkness falls, light your lamp and the beast will become as alive as you see him now.'

'OK!' Jack nodded firmly, before he had time to change his mind. 'OK! I'll do it. I'll find Saleem and Mercedes and, what was it … a jewelled box? I haven't a clue how I can find a small box in a strange place, but I'll give it a go. It'll be cool, like an adventure, as long as no one guesses I'm not the real Jack Burnside.'

'No one will guess, my Lord Burnside. Sleep now, for you are tired and, after you have slept your fill, I will take you to the palace.'

Chapter Five

The Kingdom not on a Map

Jack gazed about him eagerly as the camel trotted along the sandy track, the brown nothingness of the landscape quickly swallowing up the town of Mersham.

Jacob was perched on a saddle strapped to the camel's shoulders, while Jack was seated against its hump, his rucksack on his back and his boots, his passport into the Prince's palace, once more slung around his neck. Bud, resentful at being turned back into his wooden form, had been tucked into Jack's rucksack. Whenever Jacob spoke, he made his presence felt — although Jack hadn't a clue how he did it — by bumping against Jack's back.

'How do you know which way to go?' he asked, peering round the merchant's shoulders.

'This path I have trodden many a year, my Lord Burnside. I know every contour of the land. My faithful steed can also be trusted to move from one waterhole to another without hesitation.'

'Is that how you navigate, Jacob?'

'Indeed, my Lord. Also by the sun and the stars.'

'But what about when there's no sun?'

'There is always sun, my Lord. The sun emerges every morning and disappears every night, as we breathe in and out.'

Jack fell silent wondering what it was like to live in that hot climate, day after day. He glanced at his watch. Even though it was past four o'clock, the heat had hardly begun to drop.

On and on the sand flowed, an endless pale gold carpet, its fine particles stirred into a mist as the camel's feet broke the surface. Then, just as Jack was beginning to feel their journey would never end, gazing at a distant horizon which never altered one jot, there was a change. Mountains appeared, their path rising steeply uphill. After a short while the camel crested a small ridge and Jacob, pulling on the reins, brought it to a halt.

'Why have we stopped?' Jack stared round at the mountains towering above them like prowling giants.

'The kingdom does not lie on any map,' Jacob explained. 'It is hidden behind these mountains and can only be entered at sunset.'

As Jack watched, the majestic globe of blistering yellow, which had pursued them all day, changed from gold to orange and scarlet in the soft blue sky. Gradually, it began to slip down towards the earth, the horizon biting chunks out of it. Suddenly, a shaft of light struck the polished surface of the granite cliff and a path appeared among the rocks below.

Jacob urged the camel forward, the path disappearing into a narrow gorge between high cliffs of rock. Jack heard voices coming from above them and looked up – then wished he hadn't. He gripped the merchant's shoulder, shaking it to get his attention.

'J … J … J … Jacob,' he stuttered, staring at the twirling tip of a gleaming sword, which appeared to be making a beeline for his eyebrows.

'*Hsst*, my Lord! It will be all right, do not fear.' Jacob kept his eyes on the rock-strewn path in front of them, never even bothering to raise his head. 'These men guard the pass. They will not hurt us. Remember, I warned that you will encounter many strange things; this is but one of them.'

Jack glanced timidly at the tall, bearded man, wrapped from head to toe in a voluminous brown cloak, who was scowling at him from a ledge above his head, all the time swishing the curved blade ferociously through the air. Jacob had said a lot of things, but he was positive there'd been no mention of men with swords, he'd have remembered.

Leaving the shadowy pass behind them, they emerged on to the slopes of a green valley. Below them lay a patchwork of green fields, small stone houses dotted around like pieces on a chessboard. In the distance Jack could see sand-coloured walls, with towers like sparkling green turrets and, beyond that, a forest of domed roofs, the tallest painted gold.

'Is that the palace? Wow! It's fabulous,' Jack said, feeling a good deal more cheerful now the gloomy mountains were safely behind them.

The merchant lifted his head. 'Ah yes, it is indeed a jewel in the desert,' he said, urging the camel down the slope.

'And there's the football pitch!' Jack shouted, catching sight of a stretch of levelled turf close to the palace, its unmistakable white goalposts at each end, with a long shed-like structure, running almost the length of the pitch, its front open to the elements.

'The ground has recently been completed ready for the match,' explained Jacob. 'Naturally, this will be played at night when the heat has gone. As you see there is floodlighting.'

With the palace walls towering above them, the camel made its way along a tree-lined track. A moment later and sentries ran out to meet them. Jacob slid down from the back of the camel as the armed men surrounded them, their spear tips touching the camel's flanks.

'Salaam!' The tips of Jacob's fingers brushed his forehead.

The men spoke harshly in a language Jack had never heard before and he recognised his name, 'Jack Burnside'. The sentries turned, curiously examining him, using their spear points to touch his hair and clothing. Terrified, Jack drew in a breath, hardly daring to move a muscle as a spear touched his chest. He flinched but kept still, until one of the sentries thrust a spear menacingly into his face, indicating that he should get down.

Leaving the camel behind they walked through massive iron gates, that glinted fiercely in the rays of the setting sun, as if to warn those who entered they did so at their own peril. Jack glanced furtively about him but there was nothing to see – only an empty stone yard flanked by ramparts, along which sentries patrolled. On the far side was a second gate made of bronze, with guard towers looming over it like birds of prey. As they approached it slowly opened, allowing the party to pass through deeper into the palace grounds. Jack shivered as the thought of being swallowed alive overtook him.

They emerged into the sunlight of a wide courtyard. Here, a white marble path, bordered by grassy banks, wound through groves of flowering trees. Jack could see palm trees with bananas and dates hanging from their branches, and heard the sound of running water. There were birds, too. He caught a glimpse of a peacock and heard its raucous cry.

'Who lives here?' he whispered.

'*Hsst*, my Lord! Hold your silence, for the sentries have told us not to speak.' Jacob said softly into Jack's ear.

One of the guards turned shaking his spear menacingly at Jacob. He quickly bowed, touching his forehead in a salaam.

Jack's legs began to shake and he wished, for the umpteenth time, he was back home safe in bed – Saleem or no Saleem. But there was no escape now, not if he didn't want to be hacked to pieces. Even the guarantee from Jacob, that he would come to no harm, wasn't of much comfort, faced with spears that could easily make a nonsense of his head.

They stopped in front of a majestic-looking building, its doors studded all over with what looked like monstrous gold buttons. Silently, they swung open to reveal a vast hall lit with brilliant flashes of colour, like a medieval jousting field full of coloured tents, their walls shimmering like sunlight. Jack quickly peeped through the open flaps into the tent nearest to him, which had been decorated in shades of orange. Tasselled lanterns hung from a tented ceiling and it was furnished with long couches, low tables grouped in front of them.

A wide marble pavement ran down the centre of the hall with pillars, like gigantic oak trees, sprouting out of it, supporting the high domed roof. At the far end Jack could see a raised marble dais with a small golden dome floating above it. On it a single couch, covered with cushions in all the colours of the rainbow. It was deserted.

The massive doors silently closed behind their escort.

'We are to wait here, my Lord Burnside,' Jacob said quietly.

Somewhere, far off, Jack heard music. Hardly audible at first, it got gradually louder, as if someone out of sight was turning up the volume. *It's just like going to the dentist*, he thought and sweat broke out on his forehead trickling down his face, even though it was cool in the hall. A figure appeared, clad from top-to-toe in gold and supported on either side by servants, who led him towards the couch. At the same time Jacob's hand rose into the air. There was a puff of smoke and showers of rose petals floated down from the golden dome. When the last one had fallen, Jacob fell to his knees, touching his forehead to the ground. He tugged at Jack's sleeve but Jack abruptly pulled away, wrenching his jacket out of the clutching fingers. He glowered angrily.

'Your footballer, for I presume it is your footballer, has spirit.' A silken-tongued voice, as smooth as the silk he was wearing. 'You may speak, infidel.'

'S ... sir.' Jack's throat suddenly seized up. He cleared it, wondering what excuse he could possibly use for not crawling round the floor like a baby. 'Sir, in our country we stand in the presence of our Queen,' he guessed, crossing his fingers tightly behind his back.

'Aaaah!' As he spoke Saladin spat into a brass spittoon – twang –

the noise breaking the tension around them. 'You have done me a service, merchant. You may go.'

Jack turned helplessly to watch his only friend in this hostile place disappear, as the great wooden doors opened and swallowed him up.

'What is your name, infidel?'

'Jack Burnside, sir.'

'Aaaah, the footballer!'

Jack swallowed nervously. 'Yes! You have seen me play?' he answered hesitantly, rapidly coming to the conclusion that having all his teeth out might well be less scary than talking to Saladin.

'Briefly, briefly, but I welcome you to our land,' the smooth as silk voice went on.

Jack slowly uncrossed his fingers.

'You will be well housed here,' continued the ruler, 'and anything you require, you have only to ask. You are hungry?'

'Yes, sir.'

'We will eat and you may meet the boys.'

'*Boys*, sir?'

'Yes. It is a team of boys who will play this match. Servants, who have entered my service from the surrounding villages.'

Jack sighed and the big weight he'd been carrying around in his chest, ever since he'd stupidly said okay, suddenly got a bit smaller. Coaching kids would be *so easy*.

'And the opposition?' he said, carefully keeping his face expressionless.

'Aaaah, yes! The opposition.' The ruler almost purred as he spoke the word. 'They are a team belonging to my esteem-ed neighbour, who has the realm across the mountains. Until my spies report back, I have no idea as to their strength. But you may be assured they will be a team of cheaters and scoundrels. Now, to more pleasant things. Let us eat.'

Saladin sat up and clapped his hands, his feet sliding into gold slippers which lay side by side on the floor. Instantly, an attendant emerged from behind the gold curtains surrounding the dais, his left arm held across his eyes as if he was defending himself. He rushed to Saladin's side, offering him the arm for support.

He needs it too, thought Jack, looking at the upright Saladin. Not tall but monstrously fat, with at least three stomachs and four chins. So fat, that the attendant, no stripling himself, struggled to support his weight. Saladin moved into the scarlet tent where servants were setting out plates of food. He seated himself on one of the couches, beckoning Jack to do the same.

All around them Jack could hear people talking and laughing, but couldn't see anyone, the curtains of the scarlet tent tightly closed. He sat down and a young servant boy offered him perfumed water and a towel, so he could wash his hands.

'Are there other people here?' he asked, watching closely as the Prince began his meal, copying his manner of eating with his right hand. The food was good too; some sort of roasted meat with spices, sitting on a dish of rice and strange-looking vegetables. His stomach groaned with hunger, rumbling noisily.

'Of course, there are many people; my wives and children as well as my courtiers. They are of no consequence,' Saladin replied, stuffing his face. 'You have seen the football ground?'

'Yes, sir, on my way in.'

'And is it not magnificent? No expense was spared. At last, with your help, we can host the match in this kingdom and perhaps win.'

'I'll do my best, sir.'

'Of course you will, Mr Burnside, *for that is why you were invited.* And when you return to your country, you will be able to tell people how hospitable and civilised we are. Soon our land will be open to the world and people will flock to marvel at its wonders.' Saladin clapped his hands, belching noisily. He said something in Arabic, courteously translating his words into English. 'I have asked for the boys to be sent in.'

Jack belched, following the Prince's example and, since he was champion belcher at school, easily outdoing him in volume. The Prince acknowledged the compliment with a salaam.

The curtains parted and a boy entered. He was dressed exactly like the heroic attendant in a scarlet and gold gown, a gold turban and gold slippers. He bowed silently, his face small and insignificant under the turban and, moving across the tented room, disappeared through the curtains. After a minute another boy, exactly like the first, entered, then another and another. Jack counted ten, though it could have been one boy ten times, since they were identical in every way, even their gaze fixed unmoving on the floor.

'Excuse me, sir, is that all of them? There are only ten?'

Jack noticed the Prince hesitate and look about him. Instantly a courtier appeared in the gap between the silken folds. He said nothing but inclined his head slightly.

'Of course,' replied the Prince.

'But, sir, a football team has to have eleven players. More with substitutes,' Jack protested.

'Then you will play.'

Saladin's voice sounded sugary sweet, yet there was no doubt in Jack's mind this was an order.

'I am tired now. You are dismissed. My servant will show you to your quarters.'

Five minutes later, Jack was safely inside his bedroom, the door bolted behind him. He leaned back against its solid firmness and closed his eyes. He'd got into the palace; now, it was up to him and Bud to find Saleem.

Chapter Six

Saleem

Quickly unfastening his rucksack, Jack pulled out the wooden statue and set it on a table in front of the lamp. His fingers were itching to turn the switch but he forced himself to wait until he'd checked out his room. He pulled open the first of two identical doors which led to a bathroom, the other to a small balcony. He peeped through the window or what passed for a window, simply a large hole cut in the stone wall, wooden shutters on either side. The moon soared from behind a cloud. Catching a glimpse of one of the floodlights, Jack guessed his room was at the rear of the palace. Still, all that had to wait, he could explore another time.

Although it wasn't late, the sun had long since disappeared over the horizon, bringing instant relief from the heat and, everywhere, lights were springing up. Jack switched on his lamp and its dim rays caught the silhouette of the camel, reflecting it on to the wall. As he watched, the shadow grew and grew and, to his immense relief, a nose popped out of the wall and looked at him.

'Jeez, Bud, this has been one hell of a peculiar day and am I glad to see you.'

'If for you it has been bad …' Bud spat noisily.

'Shush! You can't spit here, you never know who's listening,' whispered Jack nervously.

The camel directed a withering glance at the boy. 'As I was saying – before you rudely interrupted me – if for you it has been bad, how many thousand times more difficult has it been for me, locked up in

44

that evil smelling-of-feet bag, doomed to listen to the caterwauling of that illegitimate son of Bathsheba, and *now* to find no food.'

'I'm sorry, but how can I ask for hay? There are dates here, look,' whispered Jack.

'I don't eat dates. However, it is fortunate I can live on my hump,' replied the camel grumpily and withdrew into the wall.

'Come on, Bud,' coaxed Jack. 'We'll try and get you some food but we've got work to do. What about Jacob's box? Will it be easy to find?'

'It is small.'

'How big is small?' Jack looked sternly at the camel.

'Certainly small enough to sit on your hand.'

'How am I going to find something that small?' he yelped. 'It could be in Saladin's pocket.'

'Saladin does not have pockets.'

'Well, anywhere then.'

'It will find you, if you fail to find it,' announced the camel, somewhat obscurely.

'Find me?' Jack clasped his head in bewilderment. 'But how can I find anything? I can't even find my way back to the hall. When that servant bloke brought me here, we came up so many stairs and passageways I lost my bearings, and now I haven't a clue where we are.'

'I, on the other hand, did not,' said Bud with great superiority and, sticking his nose out of the wall again, leered at Jack. 'I know exactly where we are. You were led round in circles or, to be more accurate, in squares – since there are no circles in the palace. But now, you will have no need to remember which of these accurs-ed halls is which, simply climb onto my back and we will search the palace like a shadow in the moonlight. None will see us.'

'You mean we'll be invisible?' said Jack, leaping off the bed in excitement.

'Yes, infidel. But hush, it is as yet early. There are many people about. Now is the time for sleep. I will wake you when the palace is quiet.'

Bud was right, even Jack had to acknowledge that. Somewhere far off he could hear music and, very faintly, sounds of talking, even of laughter. He switched out the light, leaving the room lit by stars and moonlight, the shadow of the camel on the wall a comforting sight. It would be good to sleep a little.

* * *

The shadow separated itself from the wall of the room and, with Jack on his back, moonbeams running before them to light their path, Bud strode along its rays. Jack sat cocooned among the saddle rugs, for the palace had suddenly become bitterly cold, and now an icy desert wind blew through the open windows, clearing away the last of the sun's warmth. There was no sound. It was as if no one existed, no one except him and the camel beneath him, living, breathing beings.

Silently, Bud strode down and down again, until they were underground.

'Can you see, Bud?' Jack asked curiously as the darkness began to close in.

'The darkness is my home, infidel, it is only the sun I fear, and we must be back in your room before it crosses the horizon.'

Jack yawned, wishing he was back in his room and fast asleep, right now. 'Dawn! I'll never stay awake till then. By the way, where are we going, I *thought* we were looking for the kitchen.'

'I know where the kitchen is.'

'You mean we're looking for Saleem underground? Gross! And what about Mercedes? Don't forget we have to find her as well.'

'She is not in danger, infidel, Saleem is.'

Bud, after waiting a second for a reply, moved on again, lengthening his stride as if to make up for stopping. Silently, they floated down long corridors which criss-crossed under the palace. Then, without warning, Jack could feel people on either side of them. Except they weren't people – simply presences; dark shadows groping their way round tiny caged rooms, into which the sun never shone. Jack could smell them and hear their moans and sighs, but couldn't see them. A scream of fear broke through the darkness. He shivered and, leaning forward, put his mouth to Bud's ear.

'Where are we?' he whispered.

'In the prison, my Lord Burnside. My accurs-ed master – that sometime woodcarver cum merchant cum soothsayer – told you of the depraved nature of Prince Saladin. He finds it amusing to disappear people if they offend him.'

They appeared to be passing through an immense underground prison. Jack could not begin to imagine how many men were down there but, judging from the groans and clanking of shackles, it had to be quite a number.

'Can the prisoners hear us?'

'No, my Lord, they will feel only the movement of the wind as we pass.'

'So can we rescue them?' said Jack, speaking in a normal voice.

The camel's harness let out a ringing sound as he shook his head. 'Not yet, infidel, there is more important work to do first.'

They passed on, leaving the unbearable sounds of the prison behind. 'Bud, why do you keep calling Jacob that sometime woodcarver cum merchant cum soothsayer?' Jack said. 'It takes for ever to say.'

'I should have told you, that in our land we call a man by what he does. My master is all these things and many more. *Ah*!'

Ahead of them the dim shape of a doorway appeared. It looked solid and impenetrable, until Jack realised that fragile shimmers of light were trickling through its thick wooden panels. Someone was imprisoned there, someone who had a light. The camel, with the boy seated on him, passed through the stoutly barred door; Jack almost crying out with excitement as they eased through the heavy wood as if it were butter.

The room was furnished with a bed, chairs and a table, on which Jack could see books and a chess set. It was empty. Disappointed, he slid to the ground and gazed about him frowning. Obviously the barred door had once housed a prisoner, otherwise why lock and bar the door – but why leave the light on?

A sudden noise made him glance up. Way above his head, narrow iron beams spanned the room. Swinging upside down from one of them was a boy.

Jack stared at him in amazement and called out without thinking, 'Saleem! What are you doing up there?'

The boy gasped, losing his hold on the bar and fell, recovering just in time to prevent his head smashing into the stone floor. His hands went down to take his weight; he flipped over onto his feet and stood up.

'Who's there?' he shouted, his face a nasty shade of green under its tan.

Jack stepped out of the shadows. 'Sorry, I didn't mean to startle you.'

'*Jack!*' the boy gasped. '*Startle me! Hell's Bloody Bells, Jack, that's an understatement.*' He ran over and hugged his friend. 'You're the last person I ever expected to see. What are you doing here and how did you get in my cell?'

'Peace be with you, my Lord. We have been sent to find you,' said Bud, poking his nose out of the wall.

The boy jumped as he saw the nose and laughed shakily, pushing his thick mop of dark hair out of his eyes.

'Who are you … I mean what are you? I mean … it's gotta be magic! Does that mean Jacob's behind this?

Jack nodded: 'But I'm not magic.'

'You bet your life you are, Jack, you came through a wall.'

'Wow, yes I did, didn't I?' Jack laughed. 'But what are you doing in a prison?'

'I upset my uncle so he put me behind bars.'

'Your uncle isn't Prince Saladin by any chance?' asked Jack cautiously. Saleem nodded. 'So that means you're …'

'His Highness, Prince Saleem,' said Bud.

Jack fell silent not knowing what to say.

'No big deal, Jack.' Saleem punched him lightly on the arm. He wafted his hand airily round the four walls of his cell. 'Not much of a kingdom to be prince of, is it?'

'But why didn't you say?'

'It's a long story. Let's sit down.' Saleem dragged Jack across the cell, pushing him into the only chair and plonking himself down on his bed. 'How did you know where to find me? And how did you get into the palace, my guards said no one can get in or out.'

Jack nodded. 'That's true enough, there's guards everywhere. Except, that was the easy bit – scary but easy. Jacob did it. Saladin thinks I'm the real Jack Burnside, come to coach the Prince's team for the match.'

'You're way too young to be Jack Burnside.'

'I know! Jacob fixed that too. To the enemy I look *exactly* like Jack Burnside.'

'And did he fix for you to play like him, too?' Saleem grinned.

Jack laughed. 'Didn't ask that,' he admitted.

'Well, I *want'a* play in that match, Jack. My guards told me Saladin has built a new stadium and I *want'a* see it. Can you fix that?'

'I bet I could,' said Jack, unable to resist the chance to show off. 'Except we've got to get you out of here. Football can wait. We'll take you to Jacob, you'll be safe there.'

'No way! I'm not leaving,' Saleem shook his head stubbornly.

Jack and Bud exchanged worried glances. 'Not *leaving*!' they echoed together.

'No, I'm not going anywhere till you find my farver.'

'Your father, my Lord? Is he not dead?' The camel spoke the words reluctantly.

Saleem shook his head, his dark eyes sombre.

'They told me he was, but I don't believe'em.'

Jack frowned. Getting Saleem to change his mind, once it was made up, was like trying to operate his play station without electricity – it never worked.

'So what about Mercedes?'

'Mercedes!' Saleem gazed at him in astonishment.

'You know her?'

'Course I do. She's a mate. Why's she here?'

'I don't know but I'm supposed to find her as well,' said Jack. 'By the way, do you know anything about a box?'

'No, sorry! Can I come with you to find Mercedes? I'm left alone till morning.'

Bud's harness rang out as he shook his head.

'My Lord, we will find her. But the little infidel is correct; my master will skin me alive if we do not take you to safety.'

Saleem leapt to his feet stamping his foot. 'I told you – *I'm not going anywhere* till you find my farver.' He slumped back down on the bed, angrily brushing away his tears. 'Anyway, if I disappear from my cell, what chance has he got of staying alive?'

'He's right, Bud, you know he is,' Jack said, defending his friend. 'Let him come with us *plea-se*?'

Bud stuck his head out of the wall and gazed mournfully at the two boys.

'I told that curs-ed merchant cum woodcarver cum soothsayer that hiring a christian was folly, but did he listen to me?' He spat noisily. '*Pfliipt!*'

Jack grinned triumphantly. 'In case you don't know, Saleem, that means yes.'

Saleem leapt to his feet and stopped dead staring at the wall, a puzzled expression on his face.

'But how do you get on a shadow?'

Jack laughed. 'That's easy. Hang on a mo' and Bud'll do his favourite trick.' Saleem watched as the camel strolled out of the wall, acquiring a hairy coat and knobbly knees on the way.

'Now that's what I call magic,' he said and, looking more cheerful, swung himself into the saddle in front of Jack.

The camel, with its two riders, moved softly through the cell wall.

'Where to first, my Lord?' Bud asked.

'Can anyone see us?' Saleem whispered.

'No, my Lord,' said the camel, the bells on his harness ringing out merrily as he bowed his head. 'I remain a shadow in the moonlight, unless I wish to be seen.'

'OK! First, I'll show you round the palace, then I need some food; I'm starving.'

'But what about Mercedes?' said Jack, gazing at Saleem's thin back. He might make a joke about things but he wasn't joking about being starving.

'It's cool. I know where she'll be and, you can bet your life, she's fine. Never known Mercedes anyfing else. You can get her tomorrow; my farver is much more important.'

* * *

With Saleem as guide, the party quickly found themselves outside in the fresh air. Jack, looking about him, hoped fervently Bud would remember the shortcut, the thought of passing through the dungeons again made him feel sick.

Saleem led the party along the wide stone courtyard, steadily searching every room, all of them quite plainly not concealing anything. Then Bud swam through the heavy bronze gate, entering the inner courtyard with its trees and soft grass. On one side of the quadrangle there were kitchens and offices and, in front of them, the palace proper. A massive stone building, it surged out of the perimeter wall, flowing into the garden like the tentacles of a multi-armed octopus. As if to emphasise their importance, the staterooms, with their high domed-roofs and carved doors, had guards posted in front of them – guards, who were now sleeping peacefully. And, plainly visible from every side of the courtyard, the gold dome of the great hall where Jack had dined.

'My farver built that, not Saladin,' said Saleem bitterly. 'I call it the Rainbow Hall, my favourite's the purple tent.'

Jack glanced at the tired-looking face in front of him. 'You'll get it back, Saleem. I just know you will,' he said, trying to sound more confident than he really felt.

After an hour, even Saleem gave up. They had gone into so many rooms that Jack felt dizzy.

'Saleem,' he whispered. 'Food and sleep or I'll look like you.'

Within five minutes they were in the kitchens. Saleem found fresh hay in one of the store rooms for Bud, who munched noisily, while they picked at the remnants of the evening meal.

'Good job the cooks are lazy and don't throw out the food straight after the evening meal, like they're s'posed to do,' said Saleem, chewing on a piece of barbecued lamb.

'How do you know Jacob, Saleem?'

'My farver and Jacob have been friends for years, ever since Jacob saved his life.'

'How?'

'Saladin's my farver's younger brother. Farver rarely spoke of him, except to warn me he was evil. Can you believe I never met him, till he turned up here? When my grandfarver died, our custom is for any money to go to the eldest son but my farver wanted to share his inheritance wiv his brother.' Saleem shrugged. 'Problem was Saladin wasn't happy wiv a half-share, he wanted the lot. And to make sure he got it, he only went and left Farver to die in the desert. And he would'ave too, if Jacob hadn't come along.'

Bud spat noisily: '*May Saladin be curs-ed for what he has done to Prince Salah!*'

Saleem laughed. 'Dead right, Bud.'

'Why do all your names begin with S? It's real confusing.'

'Family tradition,' explained Saleem. 'Anyhow after Mover died, Jacob came to live in the palace and I got to go to school wiv Mercedes. Then I was sent to Birming'um, to friends of Farver's, to learn English. That's how I got to join the junior league at Aston Villa.'

'But why didn't you tell me you were a prince?'

'And be treated differently? No thanks. I wanted to be like everyone else. Then, last summer, somefing happened and I was whisked back here.' Saleem stopped.

'And?'

He shrugged. 'Did you know the whereabouts of the kingdom were kept secret?'

Jack shook his head. 'No, but Jacob said you could only enter it at sunset.'

Saleem nodded. 'That's right. Jacob hid the kingdom so Saladin couldn't find us. No one knew where it was until, one night, we found soldiers pouring into the courtyard. Someone had betrayed the secret.'

'Who?

'My money's on Mendorun, I haven't any proof but ...'

'Who's he?'

'The local warlord. Has the place next door so to speak, which to you is just over the mountains, near Tigrit.' Saleem paused. 'Now he's somefing else! Winning the football match? Don't bother – he'll fix it, even if you have to disappear.'

A cold finger of fear ran down Jack's spine. '*Disappear, all because of a football match!* You can't be serious. Go on, what happened then?'

'Saladin hustled me out of the palace. Told me my farver's enemies were behind the attack and he'd been killed. I didn't believe him then and I don't now. I'm positive I was kept in Mendorun's fortress, though I never saw him. Then, a few weeks ago, I was brought back here. Saladin told me I'd be reinstated if I accepted him as rightful ruler. I wasn't having that and I accused him of being a treacherous, lying bastard.' Saleem shrugged. 'So he locked me up until I saw the error of my ways.'

'And Jacob?'

'He wasn't here. They'd been rumours of men gathering in Tigrit. Farver sent him to check out what was going on. He might be magic but his crystal ball didn't help us this time.'

'Well, if you believe your father's alive, we'll keep searching till we find him.' Jack looked at his watch. 'Jeez! It's gone two and I have to get up in four hours. *Please* change your mind and go to Jacob's.'

Saleem moved towards the camel and mounted up. He shook his head. 'I'm staying to help. Anyhow, now you're here, it won't seem a bit like being in prison. My farver's alive, I just know it. And, once we've found him, we'll all go.'

Chapter Seven

Football in Bare Feet

A furious thumping on the door brought Jack to his senses. He groaned and muttered something that sounded to him like, 'come in'. The door opened and a white-garbed servant entered the room. Jack squinted blearily through one eye, which seemed to have a will of its own and kept closing again.

'Salaam Aleikoum!'

'Salaam … Aleikoum?' muttered Jack tentatively. 'You can put it there,' he added, waving a hand at the tray the man was carrying. Breakfast! He slid quickly out of bed, suddenly wide-awake.

'Shrukran,' he stuttered, as the man put the tray down.

The servant turned towards him grinning and launched into a torrent of Arabic.

'No, no, I don't understand.' Jack waved his arms furiously.

The servant stopped and pointed at Jack's shirt and jeans, making a pantomime of washing them.

Jack laughed. 'OK!' he nodded.

The man held up a white tunic and clean underwear.

'NO!' Jack waggled both hands violently in the air and pointed to the underwear. Thank goodness, his mum had spent half her life lecturing him, on the wisdom of keeping a spare set in his football bag. He wouldn't be caught dead in those old-fashioned jobs.

The man grinned again and, picking up Jack's dirty clothes, went out closing the door behind him.

Jack glanced up at the wall expecting to see the shadow of the camel. Panicking he called out then laughed shakily. Of course it was broad daylight. He looked down.

'You can't stay here, Bud,' he said, picking up the small statue and putting it in his bag. 'I need my ticket home with me at all times and, as soon as I've eaten, we're off to football.'

His room was quite bare, its walls and ceiling of plain whitewashed stone, its floor made from tiny coloured squares of marble which were cool to walk on. There was nothing much in it except for a bed, bedside table and a large chest for his clothes. He had been surprised to find electricity, although the lamp by his bed had a weird type of switch, the knob turning round and round instead of a push-on, push-off.

Streams of sunlight trickled through the carved balcony doors. He didn't bother to open them, promising himself to do that when he got back from training, although he'd explored the small bathroom the night before. At least everything worked, even if the shower was incredibly old-fashioned; a concrete shower stall – no curtains – the water spraying out of a metal pipe clipped to the ceiling. And the loo – simply a hole in the tiles next to the shower, with flat foot rests.

It'll do, he thought, washing thoroughly but fast, since his stomach was already growling at the thought of breakfast.

The tray was full of food; milk to drink, bread, a type of yoghurt, honey, and fruit, just enough to keep him going till lunch. There was a lot to think about and eating helped.

He'd worked his way through the whole tray, leaving nothing behind except a scraping of honey and a couple of dates, when there came a loud knock on his door. Another servant and, by the way he was waving his arms, Jack knew he had to follow. He collected his rucksack, looping it over his arm. Strangely the tunic felt comfortable. It was cool and loose and, since everyone else was wearing the same, he didn't feel too bad about it. Anyway, it was only until his jeans were washed. He tried stretching his legs. Good, he could still run if he had to.

This time he knew exactly where he was going, grinning to himself as the servant dutifully led him the long way round, finally ending up on the ground floor. Turning away from the trees and fountains, the man dived into a narrow gap between two buildings, emerging in the outer courtyard at the rear of the palace. Pointing to a small door in the heavy rock wall, he opened it with a bow. Next moment, Jack was outside the palace walls.

The morning air was fresh and cool, although Jack suspected it would heat up pretty quickly. He trotted across the grassy space and opened the barred gate, the football stadium clearly visible on the far side of the low wall. Instantly at home, he made his way across the ground into the stand, the servant following him closely. After inspecting the locker room, he changed into his kit. Wearing his new ManU number 7 shirt, he walked noisily back up the paved steps, his studs making their usual thrilling clatter. The covered stand ran almost the length of the pitch but by English standards it was quite small, with only half-a-dozen tiered rows, and it was completely empty.

'Am I too early?' he asked, looking pointedly at his watch.

The manservant shrugged.

Jack clattered down the steps to one of four benches and sat down, his rucksack on the bench beside him. The palace looked peaceful in the early morning light making it difficult to believe the murder and mayhem Saleem had spoken about. A solitary sentry patrolled the ramparts nearest to him, his route taking him between two towers, arrow slits plainly visible in their walls. It was definitely well fortified.

'S'pect they use boiling oil to destroy their enemies, 'cos there isn't much water in the desert,' he muttered. He grinned at the servant who stood near by, wishing he could speak English so he could share the joke.

Abruptly, the gate at the far side of the ground opened and a series of bodies tumbled through, as if tossed there by some passing giant. For a moment they remained motionless, huddled together in their long, white tunics, like christians thrust into the arena to be eaten by lions. Next second, they charged across the pitch screaming and shouting. Jack leapt to his feet, trying to keep his balance as they circled round him, buffeting him with their elbows, reverently touching his shirt and fingering the ball which he'd got firmly clasped in his arms.

'Football, football, football,' they chanted excitedly.

Luckily, he was by far the tallest and they were all different shapes and sizes, not identical at all. He recognised the boy who had worn the gold turban and tunic the night before, and grinned at him.

'Good morning!' he said, gazing in dismay at the ten pairs of bare feet in front of him – no shorts or t-shirts either.

'Salaam Aleikoum,' they chorused.

'First, let's see you run.'

Silence!

'Run,' said Jack, running up and down on the spot.

Nothing happened.

'Follow me,' he shouted and set off across the pitch.

Nothing happened again, except the ten boys shifted uneasily from one foot to another.

'Is there anyone here who speaks English?' A feeling of doom struck Jack. Now what was he to do? Jacob had forgotten all about the language problem.

A loud thud broke the silence. Startled, Jack glanced up to see the gate flying open. It crashed back against the wall and guards appeared, two of them holding the gate wide, allowing a palanquin carried by four heavily built men to pass through. On it sat the Prince and by his side walked a group of retainers, among them Saladin's armrest from the night before. Instantly, the ten boys fell to the ground, their faces hidden in the dust, although Jack, remembering his words of the previous day, stayed standing. Then, deciding something was needed, he inclined his head in a small bow.

'Aaaah, Mr Burnside, it is good to see you are so eager. However, please remember that *nothing* starts without my permission.'

The words seemed friendly enough, although there was menace in the silvery tones that sent shivers down Jack's spine. He understood instantly that no one, *but no one*, disobeyed an order.

'I'm sorry, sir, I didn't know.'

'Of course not,' said Prince Saladin, his voice silky-smooth, waving away the problem with a flutter of his hand. 'Now, you may begin.'

'Sir, none of the boys speak English, I'll need an interpreter,' Jack admitted.

'Nothing simpler, Mr Burnside. You go.' Saladin turned to one of his courtiers and pointed. The man salaamed. Saladin waved his hand and the procession pursued its ponderous way into the shade of the stand. Jack watched mesmerised at the antics of the men trying to lower the platform to the ground with Saladin still on it.

'OK! Let's run,' he shouted. 'Across the pitch and back, nice steady jog.'

'Please?' asked the interpreter.

'Do you speak English?' said Jack.

'Yes, sir. Please to speak slowly.'

'OK! Tell the boys to run – not fast – across the pitch. Two times.'

A torrent of Arabic greeted his words, several of the boys running wildly across the pitch, others chasing after them. Jack set off in pursuit.

'Stop,' he yelled waving his arms.

The runners stopped in mid-flight, looking back at him. He turned round to find his interpreter, only to see him cross to the bench and sit down.

'I need you here,' he shouted.

'Sir?'

'*Here!*'

'Yes, sir,' said the man, walking slowly towards him.

'Prat!' muttered Jack, patting the air with his hands. 'Wait here.'

He needed an interpreter and a good one at that. He ran over to the stand where Saladin was sitting. Time for some major sucking up. He bowed low, plastering his face with a gushing smile. 'Prince Saladin, may I trouble you again?'

Saladin waved his hand.

'I expect I am worrying you unnecessarily,' Jack took a huge breath. 'As I expect your interpreter is just temporary – I expect you have already noticed I need an interpreter who can run. Er … preferably … er … someone younger who speaks English and plays football. But … er … I expect you have already thought of that and I'm worrying you unnecessarily.' *Phew!* He wiped the sweat off his brow.

Saladin studied him closely for a minute without saying anything, his eyes never leaving Jack's face. Then he beckoned to his armrest, who ran up bowing, and some furious-sounding words were exchanged. Still shouting, the ruler pointed to one of the servants, prompting the man to flee towards the palace. Obviously still not satisfied, he rounded on his courtiers shouting at them in turn, each one salaaming at the beginning and end of his speech. He swung back to Jack.

'You are quite right, Mr Burnside. There is *someone*.' Saladin hissed. 'You are quite correct; I had already noticed that you were experiencing difficulties in communicating your instructions. Wait please,' he said smoothly.

Jack gave a smile of thanks meeting Saladin's eyes. He recoiled, scarcely concealing the shudder that ran through him as the black, soulless, unblinking, expressionless pits bored into him. The shouting was better.

Turning his back Saladin began chatting in a friendly fashion to the man seated next to him, ignoring Jack completely. He stared round at the surrounding hills, nervously wondering what he would do if his plan didn't work. Above them the sky was empty, not a single cloud – nothing except for a lone bird hovering overhead, its wings outstretched, floating in the currents of air, hardly moving at all. He heard the gate click and turned eagerly. Guards appeared, escorting a small figure walking between them. *Saleem*!

'So he comes,' hissed Saladin, looking up.

Jack watched, as Saleem bowed to the man who had stolen his father's throne. There was some talk, silky in tongue from the ruler, Saleem only answering, 'Aiwa', as the Prince finished speaking.

'This boy is a criminal from our dungeons. He can do what you want. However, he is only permitted to answer questions on football. *Do I make myself clear?*' Again the words were softly spoken.

Saleem raised his head as if to say something, and then, just as quickly, looked down at the ground.

'Yes, sir, thank you,' said Jack, with a nod. In any other circumstances he would have grinned and shouted – but not here. He kept his mouth firmly shut, never even looking at Saleem. Time enough to talk, when they met that night in the safety of Saleem's cell. 'What do I call you?' he asked.

'Ss …'

'You call him Ali,' said Saladin, smoothly interrupting.

'Er, Ali, can you play football?'

'You bet.'

'OK! Tell the team to jog across the pitch two times.'

The training session began again with Saleem explaining what Jack wanted, so easily and quickly it made Jack look quite good – almost like a professional. After the run, Jack started the obligatory set of warm up exercises, with stretches and shuttle runs, even though several of their audience were already using fans. When they stopped to rest and drink some water, he looked across at Saladin. Upset, the man hissed a lot, leaning forward on one arm to stare at the offender. Now, he lolled back in his seat. Yep, he was satisfied. He glanced across at Saleem. He was bent over studying the ground so Jack couldn't see his face. Just then he lifted up his cup to take a sip of water and Jack caught sight of his thumb. It was tilted backwards – *it's great* – it said.

Jack grinned. 'OK! Let's get going again. We'll try five-a-side.'

He tried to speak slowly, allowing time for translation, even though he knew Saleem would guess what he was going to say long before he said it. He explained how they would use a shorter pitch and only play ten minutes each way, pointing out the makeshift goal at one end, which he'd marked with his spare shirt and trainers.

'Ali, tell the boys they can have a go at everything and we'll see where they play best.'

Saleem nodded.

'Anyone like playing in goal?'

Four hands shot up. Jack pointed to two of them.

'That's Iqbal and that's Ahmed,' said Saleem helpfully, as the boys grinned and saluted.

'And midfield, I'll have you and you.'

'Hassan and Omar,' added Saleem.

'Yes, that's right,' said Jack. 'Iqbal – Ahmed – Hassan – Omar,' he muttered, fixing their names in his brain then, giving up on the others, gave them numbers.

He couldn't have asked for better, even if he had been Jack Burnside. The boys might have been small and thin, but they were fit and strong and obviously loved the game. Growing up barefooted had given them toes of iron, so they had no problems handling the light ball. And they didn't argue, just got on with it. But, even without any skill as a coach, Jack knew he had his work cut out to get them ready for a match. Their long tunics were difficult to play in and their knowledge of rules non-existent. Jack watched with dismay as one the youngsters stopped dead, looked round at the other players before aiming the ball at the goal.

'Isn't that Iqbal?' he shouted to Saleem. 'I thought he was in goal?'

'He is,' Saleem grinned mischievously.

Jack groaned and reached for his whistle, deciding at the last moment to let it go and work out any problems at the next session.

Training lasted two hours and when Saladin stood up, effectively stopping any further play, Jack was almost grateful, for by now the sun was high in the sky and it was quite hot. Saladin beckoned Jack, who ran over.

'You will come down again to train when the sun drops. After the session it would please me greatly if you will dine with me,' he said and bowed courteously.

'Thank you, sir.'

As Saladin's armrest took the weight of the ruler, he turned to the guards. Again there was a loud exchange. Four of them surrounded Saleem, their spears pricking his robe as they marched him off.

'Prince Saladin?'

The ruler paused.

'May I have the interpreter back? He was very helpful.'

The Prince nodded as he stepped on to the platform and was hoisted into the air.

Right, Saleem's out. One day down, five to go. Jack grabbed his rucksack and went to change.

* * *

Dinner that night was served in the orange room. Jack, seated on pale orange cushions, pushed back his shoulders feeling heaps better than he had that morning. Now he could admit to being scared stiff about pretending to be the real Jack Burnside. Keeping his eyes firmly on his plate, he waited for Saladin to start up a conversation. He eyed the tons of food in front of him greedily, even though there was way more than he and Saladin could eat. Nevertheless, he set to in good heart to munch his way through as much as possible.

Saladin lounged against cushions of pale apricot, again wearing the gold tunic and slippers, as colossal as ever.

'Do you consider, Mr Burnside, that the boys of this realm will have a chance?'

Jack looked up. 'Yes,' he replied honestly. 'They learned a lot today and they're well used to running about and are quite fit. Of course,' he said and paused.

'Of course?' put in the silver-tongued ruler, very softly.

'They'd be better if they had the proper kit.'

'What do you mean by kit?'

'Shorts and shirts, with their numbers on, and boots, if possible, or trainers.'

'Trainers! I do not know what are these trainers?'

'These.' Jack stuck out his foot. On arriving back at his room after evening practice, he'd discovered his jeans, shirt and clean underwear and, after a shower, had put them on instantly feeling much more himself.

'Ah yes, trainers. It may be possible,' Saladin purred, ladling food into his mouth.

Jack didn't blame him, for the food was good. The meat, served on a bed of rice and vegetables, tasted exactly like the kebabs he ate in England – hot and spicy, just the way he liked them. Even the hot pita bread was the same.

There was silence as Saladin tucked into some fresh meat, belching heavily. Jack followed suit.

'It is good you like our food.'

'It's great food, sir, honestly.'

'Is there anything else?' The cold eyes stared at him.

A breeze stirred the curtains of the orange tent making Jack shiver and, for a moment, he wondered if he had given himself away. 'What do you mean, sir?' he asked innocently.

'Do you wish for anything else?'

Jack shook his head, slowly letting out the breath he'd been holding. 'I don't think so, but there is something worrying me.'

'And that is?'

'Yesterday, you said your spies hadn't reported back about your neighbour's team. Is it possible he has spies here? If so, he already knows you've got a coach for your team.'

The eyes blinked and the hand, poised to thrust more food into his mouth, paused as Saladin took in Jack's words.

'Mr Burnside, it would appear that you think as well as play football. However, I am entirely satisfied that no one has entered my household unannounced in the last few days. Yet, you are correct to be concerned. I will set more guards whilst you are training to make doubly sure.'

Chapter Eight

Mercedes

A great silver moon sailed majestically across the sky as Bud, with Jack on his back, made his way to the hidden gate leading directly to Saleem's prison. They passed easily through it and down the steeply sloping corridor, entering the cell through its wall.

Saleem was swinging from the bars. He dropped lightly to the floor and rushed over to hug Jack.

'You really are somefing else, Jack,' he said, patting his friend on the back. 'You actually got me out, I still can't believe it.' He laughed excitedly. 'I tell you what though – am I hungry! No one thought of slipping me some extra food, even though I'd spent half the day running round a football pitch. But I feel great. How did you fix it?'

Unable to get a word in edgeways, Jack climbed back in the saddle and, leaning down, hauled his friend up behind him.

'Bud, we'd better get the Prince something to eat, before he fades away with all this talking,' he laughed.

'Yes, my Lord Burnside. Certainly the eating may stem the noise, which would be an unasked for blessing.'

'No! Food can wait. Let's get searching and I know where to start,' exclaimed Saleem eagerly. 'There's some larders across from the kitchen, let's try them.' Bud, performing his party trick, walked straight through the heavy stonewalls into a shadowy corridor running parallel to the kitchens. There locked doors opened up into a series of underground larders, the impenetrable stone keeping them cool all year round. They were dark, but not the dense blackness of the dungeons, moonlight creeping in through small windows set high up in the wall. They searched, discovering an old bread stove in one; in another, joints of meat hung from hooks, and there were sacks of rice and flour in a third. In one, cheese and milk were cooling on a marble slab and in yet another, firewood was stored. As the search went on, each time drawing a blank, Saleem got quieter and quieter.

'Saleem, it's no good, we've looked everywhere – twice,' Jack said firmly. 'Head back to the kitchen, Bud, we'll get something to eat and plan our next move.'

The kitchen was huge with hundreds of pots and pans lying everywhere.

Well it has to be, Jack thought, remembering the number of people he'd seen that night in the Rainbow Hall. One complete wall was taken up by a vast fireplace, with huge ovens flanking it. The fire was low now and burned quietly. Above it, hanging from the chimney breast, were thick metal rods that slotted into the heavy iron stanchions on either side of the fire place, which were used for roasting a sheep or a cow.

He slipped off the camel's back and headed for the table groaning with food, wondering where they kept the refrigerator. He hadn't seen one anywhere; neither had they passed a supermarket on their journey to the palace, so how did the cooks manage to make the food taste so delicious?

'But we *can't* give up, I'm positive he's alive,' Saleem said stubbornly, picking at some meat and rice.

'I believe you,' said Jack, 'but instead of wasting more time, let's go get Mercedes. It's my job to find her, remember. P'rhaps she'll know something.'

Saleem's face lit up like a beacon. 'That's a great idea, why didn't I think of it. Mercedes is dead tricky, if anyone knows anyfing, it'll be her.'

'Is it not strange to you, infidel, that the one word father and daughter have in common is tricky,' said Bud.

Saleem grinned at Jack, his cheerfulness restored. 'He doesn't rate Jacob, does he,' he said, nodding at Bud.

Bud snorted contemptuously.

'Ignore'im, he's always grouchy when he's hungry,' Jack replied carelessly.

'Allow me to make a small observation, my Lord Burnside,' said the camel. 'If you continue to eat in the manner which you have shown this evening, you will shortly resemble our beloved ruler. Then only one of you will fit my saddle.'

Jack hastily dropped his spoon. He'd been absentmindedly spooning a delicious concoction of dates, mangoes, nuts and honey into his mouth, licking his lips between spoonfuls. He looked down at the empty bowl in front of him then at his legs. They hadn't changed, they remained as skinny as ever.

'OK! Point taken,' he grinned. 'Let's go.'

Leaving behind the mess of food on the huge table, Bud, with the two boys on his back, strode silently out into the moonlit courtyard. The moonlight shining on the fronds of palm trees had turned them from green to silver and water, gushing from the numerous fountains, sparkled like diamonds. Looking about him, Jack thought how lucky Saleem had been to have this garden to play in when he was growing up.

It was by now the middle of the night and, like the previous one, guards had fallen asleep. The camel, with his two riders, walked quietly between them before vanishing into the thick wood of the harem doors.

It wouldn't have mattered if the guards had been awake, thought Jack triumphantly, as the wood closed around him, *they still wouldn't have seen us.* They emerged into an anteroom, empty except for a fountain gurgling away, the moonlight bright enough to pick out patterns on the mosaic tiles. At the far end an archway, swathed in gauze curtains, gave them a glimpse of the main room beyond. Saleem stretched out a hand to pull the flimsy material to one side, as Bud, never pausing, strode through them. The room was littered with couches. On several of them women lay sleeping.

'Who lives here?' whispered Jack, glimpsing flowers growing over a circle of arches in the middle of the room. The moonlight had turned them white and they filled the room with a sweet perfume. Behind the arches, a stray moonbeam sparkled on a ripple of water.

'Saladin's wives and children,' said Saleem, 'and there's still a few of the women who used to serve my farver and stayed on as servants,' he added. 'Some were born here and have nowhere else to go and, sometimes, the wives of courtiers visit. It's a nice place.'

He pointed to the side rooms, tucked away in the shadows. Silently, Bud trod through the sleeping forms and entered one of the rooms through its wall. Several children lay sleeping. Saleem shook his head and Bud backed out.

A half-open door beckoned and they peered round it. A girl was asleep on the bed, her hair dark and curly.

'Is that Mercedes?' whispered Jack.

'You bet it is,' said Saleem, sliding down off the camel's back. He crept up to the bed and, putting his hand over the girl's mouth, whispered in her ear.

The girl opened her eyes. 'Sally, it's you,' she exclaimed rapturously and flung her arms round him. 'You've bin found!'

'Shu-u-sh! Of course it's me, Merk, who else would it be?' Saleem disentangled himself, staring at Mercedes sternly. 'Hell's Bloody Bells, Merk, you've got fat!'

'Hey, who's that?' Mercedes pointed at the door. 'Oh Great

Lucifer! It's that beast and who for cotton-pickin'-sakes is that? OK! What's Pops up to?'

'He sent us to rescue you, Oh Light of the Nile,' the camel said, calmly entering the small room. He leered down at Mercedes and, buckling his front legs, his back legs splayed outwards, deliberately sat down. Jack, still in the saddle, lurched drunkenly forwards over his neck and then jolted backwards, rather like a boxer receiving a right and left to the head.

'Don't light of the Nile me, you foul-smellin' beast. Anyway, I'm not comin',' growled Mercedes.

'But Jacob sent us to get you.' Jack stared unbelieving at the tall girl in her gaily coloured robe. How could this be Jacob's daughter? He was short and she was already a head taller than Saleem.

'And you are?' she asked suspiciously.

'I'm Jack Burnside.'

'The footballer? You can't be!'

'Er … ' began Jack.

'That's debatable,' interrupted Bud sarcastically. 'And – female member of an accurs-ed race – you can be sure I am not dragging myself into this den of iniquity, to oblige that curs-ed merchant cum woodcarver cum soothsayer, for you to tell me you are not going to be rescued.'

'I haven't found the box, so there. *And* Saladin wants to marry me.'

'Merk, you're joking. *Saladin!*'

'Marry you!' exclaimed Jack. 'You're too young. How old are you?'

'I'm almost fourteen. How old are you?'

'I'm … that's none of your business, but you can't marry that fat old man.'

'No, you can't, Merk. It's prepost'rous.'

Mercedes giggled. 'Silly, Sally.'

Saleem frowned. 'Don't call me that, I keep telling you I hate it.'

Mercedes stuck out her tongue. 'Well then, that's why I've got fat. Saladin doesn't like me now. But if I've *got* to be rescued, I can go on a diet.'

'*Where is the box*, oh accurs-ed child of Satan?' said the camel.

'Ho! I don't know, do I,' retorted Mercedes, her tone fierce. 'I've tried all the usual places. If you're that clever, then you find it, you cretinous old ...'

'Shush, Merk.' Saleem shook the girl's arm. 'Why do you have to get so riled up? Calm down will you. You may not like the beast, but he's our ticket out'a here.'

'I go along with that,' added Jack. 'One minute we're creeping around trying to be quiet and the next, there's a full scale battle going on between you and Bud. We'll wake up one of the women with all this noise.'

'Huh, you could have a battle in here and *still* no one would wake up.'

'How come?' said Jack.

'I think his wives drug themselves up to the eyeballs every night, so they're asleep before Saladin.' Mercedes shuddered dramatically. 'Sensible, I call it with that creep about.'

'Get serious, Merk, we need your help. We have to find my farver.'

'Isn't he in the dungeons with you, Saleem?' Mercedes seated herself cross-legged on her couch, her tone instantly changing to one of concern.

Saleem shook his head. 'They said he was *dead* but I don't believe'em, I *know* he's alive somewhere. But where?' he said despondently. 'We've searched everywhere. Is there anyfing you've heard? You know how women gossip.'

'Can't think of anythin' offhand.'

'Please, Merk?'

'All right! *All right!* I'll think about it. Now, as to leavin'... you camel-brains,' she said glaring at Bud, 'know as well as I do, we can't leave without the box.'

'*For crying out loud, will someone tell me what this box looks like?*' Jack exploded impatiently

'You'll know it when you see it,' Mercedes replied casually.

Jack groaned and held his head in his hands. This was like his worst nightmare – a box which he couldn't find, but which he'd know if he ever did find it.

'Well if you can't help, Merk, we'll just have to keep trying.' Saleem's tone was glum and his eyes had lost their sparkle.

'Hang on a mo, I'll get dressed and come with you.' Mercedes leapt off her bed. She draped a shawl over her shoulders and arms, pushing her feet into slippers. 'I'm not stayin' here, while you two have all the fun.'

Jack stared. It was freezing outside and both he and Saleem were wearing jackets. Mercedes' shawl was like gossamer.

'You can't come with us, it's far too dangerous for a girl,' he said somewhat unwisely.

Mercedes glared. 'Girl, huh! I can beat Saleem up any day. Ask him, he'll tell you. So I'm goin'. I might even be some help.'

'Excuse me,' interrupted Bud. 'It is I – the beast of burden – who decides if the fat-filled carcass of a girl can come with us. I doubt whether even I, as strong as I am, could carry a third person, especially one of such gigantic proportions.'

'*Why you …*'

'Bud, we can't do this without you, but please try not to insult Mercedes,' Jack said, trying not to laugh. *Wow! Fat-filled carcass! Wicked!* He could just imagine the uproar if he dared come out with that at school.

Saleem laughed out loud, his eyes sparkling brightly again. 'Oh, don't worry about Merk, she learned to trade insults from a master.

Jack didn't mean anyfing by it, Merk; he doesn't know you like I do. You're as tough as any boy. Now will you stay put?' Mercedes continued to glare. 'OK! OK! *Tougher* – satisfied?'

'Saleem's right, Mercedes. It's just … ' stuttered Jack lamely, 'I mean … with three of us moving round the palace, there's more chance of being spotted.'

'You stay then. You don't know anythin' about the palace.'

'For the sake of my farver and the men in prison; p*lease*, Merk.'

Bud jolted back onto his feet, Jack clinging tightly to the saddle to stop himself sliding off.

'May the gods preserve us! There is so much hot air blowing around this room but if it will keep you, most precious jewel of the Nile, safely tucked up in bed, may I be struck dead if I pass insults – like wind from my body – towards you again.'

'Thank you, Bud, I accept your apology and I'll stay.' Mercedes smiled disarmingly all round, and took off her shawl. 'Actually, Sally, I've been thinkin'.'

'What about?'

'Well,' said the girl eagerly. 'Don't you remember one of the larder rooms had a trap door down to a cellar, where they used to store ice? Did you check there?'

'Nice one, Merk! I'd forgotten all about that. Come on, Jack, let's go right now and see.' Saleem got to his feet.

'No way, Saleem, it's too late.'

'But we've got to, Jack, it won't take long,' he argued.

'And there's football in the morning, remember? We need sleep.'

'OK!' Saleem said miserably. 'I know it makes sense, Jack. It's just …' He shrugged. 'We'll see you tomorrow, Merk, and in the meantime …'

'Yeah, yeah, if I remember anythin' else …' She threw her arms round Saleem's neck. 'Now you take care and *you*, Jack Burnside.

Camel, you'd better see no harm comes to them or I'll tell Pops,' she said, whacking Bud hard on his rump, making him jump. 'And *don't*, for one instant, think I believed the bit about not insultin' me again. Don't forget I know you, you cantankerous old fart.'

Jack gasped.

'Always the last word,' grinned Saleem, as Jack leant down to pull him into the saddle. 'We'll be back tomorrow, just be patient.'

'If you don't come back, you'll hear about it, 'cos I'll come lookin'.'

Her belligerent tone followed them out of the room, so they missed the whispered, 'You take care now,' as they vanished through the wall and disappeared from view.

Chapter Nine

The Prisoner

'You must eat first,' Jack argued, when he collected Saleem from his cell the following night. 'You don't look as if you've had a thing all day,' he added, inspecting his friend, who appeared thinner than when he'd first seen him, two days earlier.

'But we haven't got long, Jack, it's gone midnight, we can't afford to waste a second.'

'Excuse me, my Lord Saleem. But I, the beast of burden, would appreciate a little consideration. I don't expect much, a few minutes to graze some hay and drink some water. It is a small thing to ask in return for my many gifts – such as walking through walls like a shadow, so you may safely search for Prince Salah.'

Jack laughed. 'There you are, Saleem. No contest. We go to the kitchen. Anyway, after all the exercise we've had today, you must be starving. I know I am and I've had dinner.'

Minutes later they were back in the kitchen, leaving Jack with the weirdest feeling that the palace had shrunk. He felt so weary from lack of sleep his mind had to be playing tricks.

They started searching the larder nearest the kitchen door but drew blank and started again. Again, they drew blank and yet again, each time feeling more and more despondent. Now, there were only two rooms left and they'd looked into both of these before. The first housed only brushwood for kindling the kitchen fire, and a great pile of it covered the stone floor.

'I can't see the floor,' whispered Saleem. 'Can you?'

Jack shook his head and slid to the ground. All he could think of was getting Saleem safely back to his cell and him to his bed. He felt so nervous, his stomach had wrapped itself into knots. If they got caught, he'd have a fine time trying to explain how Saleem had got out of an impenetrable dungeon. Darting across to the pile of brushwood he tried to lift it but it didn't budge.

'It's too heavy,' he whispered, tugging at the wood again. 'Give me a hand.'

Cautiously, they pulled at the bundle. There was a sudden grinding noise and, to Jack's horror, the floor beneath his feet tilted moving sharply downwards. He felt his feet slip and lunged forward, grabbing a handful of brushwood, only to hear the dry sticks snapping under his fingers, like a volley of firecrackers. His feet met air as the stone vanished from under him. In desperation, he grabbed a handful of Saleem's tunic and held on, praying the cloth wouldn't tear.

'Your hand, Jack, give me your hand,' whispered Saleem, trying not to make any noise.

Jack caught the outstretched hand as his feet fell into space and, with a jolt, his body followed. Losing his grasp on Saleem's robe, he dropped further into the darkness, the stone edge of the hole scraping the skin off his arm. He hung there, slowly revolving from side to side, his left arm flailing about in the silent air.

'Stay still.' Saleem's voice sounded panicky. 'I've got you but stop jumpin' about. I'm right on the edge here.'

'Bud?' Jack croaked.

'Infidel, I cannot reach you. My Lord Saleem speaks the truth. One false move and he will fall.'

Jack had never felt so scared in his life. He took a deep breath forcing his arm down to his side. Gradually, his body stopped swinging and hung motionless like a plumb line; his right arm, almost at breaking point, at full stretch above his head. He stared down into the darkness, imagining long, scaly fingers crawling up from the depths of the pit. He could sense them clawing at his feet, trying to drag him down. He curled up his toes in fright. Suddenly, he heard Saleem's voice.

'Jack! *Jack!* ***Jack?*** *The trapdoor, can you reach it?*'

Jack felt his shoulder blades brush against its sharp edge as Saleem hauled on his arm.

'Yes,' he whispered breathlessly.

'See if you can find somefing to hang on to,' said Saleem. 'Slowly – *Hell's Bloody Bells*, Jack – I said *slowly.*'

Jack stretched out his arm, forcing himself to move in slow motion, the cold edge of the trap door brushing against the back of his fingers. Reaching up, he tried to hook his fingers over its hard rim. They slipped off, his nails bending backwards as they scraped across the concrete, setting his body like a punch bag jolting into violent movement again. He flinched, the pain from his nails almost paralysing his hand for a minute.

'*Jack!*' hissed Saleem.

'I couldn't help it! My fingers slipped off.'

He waited until he'd stopped swinging and tried again, struggling to ignore the pain in his shoulder. Cautiously, he slid the palm of his hand over the rough surface searching for cracks but there was nothing, the stone flat and solid to his touch. Panicking, he stretched further and further. He was concentrating so hard that it was a minute or two before he realised he was pulling his body round – twisting sideways – and dragging Saleem with him. He could sense his friend straining backwards, trying to prevent both of them being toppled into the black pit.

SPACE! THERE WAS A GAP!

The air exploded out of Jack's lungs in relief as he hooked his fingers into it. By now his shoulder felt like someone was jabbing him with a red-hot needle. He desperately wanted to reach up and rub the pain away but then he might never find the gap again. Cautiously, he transferred some of his weight onto his forearm. Immediately the pain in his shoulder began to subside as the strain on it lessened. He hung silently for a moment, wondering how he could possibly get his body and legs back onto the floor.

'Saleem,' he whispered, 'if I take the weight on my left arm, can you pull me up a bit? I'll try and swing my foot up.'

There was no reply; instead, the grasp on Jack's hand tightened and he felt himself being drawn bodily upwards. With a surge of energy he kicked, willing his leg to clear the edge of the trap door. It did. Gasping with pain and out of breath, he lay spread-eagled half of him on the stone, the rest still dangling over the abyss. He lay still, trying to recover enough strength to move again.

'I'm okay, you can let go now, I can make it from here,' he murmured.

Saleem's hand cautiously released his and then silently, still without saying a word, Saleem leapt into a backwards somersault, landing on his feet well away from the edge of the hole.

Jack waited a moment longer then, pushing against the solid floor, heaved up on his arms and dragged himself away from the black pit. He collapsed face down against the hard stone, tears of relief welling up. After a second or two he got to his knees, slowly crawling out of danger and stood up.

'Jeez! That was scary! Thanks, Saleem,' he said, nodding his head painfully.

He dropped to the ground again, inching towards the edge of the hole, and peered down into the empty space. He could just make out the silhouette of a ladder vanishing into the darkness.

'What the hell, is it?' he asked.

'Not an ice cellar, that's for sure,' said Saleem, peering over his shoulder.

Jack crawled back from the edge and, getting to his feet, went over to the camel.

'Bud?'

'You are safe, effendhi?'

'Yeah, I'm okay. But how do we get down?'

Bud took two silent steps forward and put his long neck down the narrow hole, peering into the blackness.

'With difficulty, effendhi. This hole is not meant for a camel, even a magical one. I would need to find another way in.'

'There isn't time for that,' interrupted Saleem. 'Bud can stay here,' he added impatiently, his feet already reaching down to find the first step.

'No!' shouted Jack, forgetting to whisper. He clasped his hand over his mouth. 'He's our lifeline and don't you forget it.' he hissed. 'What do we need, Bud,' he said, speaking in a more normal tone, 'to get you down that hole?'

'A miracle,' said the camel, sounding very gloomy.

'But we can't stop now,' argued Saleem. 'It's the one place we haven't looked. It's gotta be worf a try.'

'There is a way to get Bud down those steps,' said Jack, thinking hard. 'Shrink him. Can you do that, Bud?'

'Of course, I can do almost anything,' said the camel, with great superiority.

'We need a lamp.'

'There's one in the kitchen,' whispered Saleem. 'Come on, Bud, quick – let's go get it. Stay here, Jack, we won't be a moment.'

The lamp was easy to light and shed a warm glow down onto steps so steep, they were almost vertical. As if on cue, Bud shrank back into his wooden statue form. Jack, picking him up, followed Saleem climbing backwards, rung by rung, down the narrow wooden steps.

'No wonder Bud said he couldn't get down here, Saleem. You have to be young, fit *and* two-legged to negotiate these steps,' he whispered, nervously staring into a well of swirling darkness below them. Jumping the last few rungs, he hastily placed the statue on the ground, lamplight reflecting its shadow onto the wall. Within seconds, the wall and ceiling were dominated by Bud's sneering face.

'Whew, am I glad to see you,' Jack admitted, as the camel emerged from the wall allowing the two boys to mount. 'We were taking one hell of a risk doing it that way. It never occurred to me, till we were half way down, that we could be seen.' He fastened the lamp to Bud's saddle to make it invisible, its light just sufficient to lift the dark shadows in front of them. 'Come on, let's get going.'

Immediately their way was barred by a stout wooden door reinforced with iron bars.

'Farver?' breathed Saleem, in Jack's ear.

Jack said nothing as the camel passed through the fortified wall. Inside, a man was sitting by the light, writing. His feet were shackled to a wall and, although he could move about the cell, it was with some difficulty against the pull of the heavy iron chain. He was very thin and bent, and looked tired.

'It's my farver. Quick, I must go to him.'

'Wait!' ordered Bud.

'What now?' Saleem cried out.

'I have not been this way before, my Lord. There may be guards within earshot. Now you know he is alive, it would be foolish to risk that life by alerting his guards. If it pleases you, my Lord, be patient a little longer.'

'*It doesn't please me, Bud.* Anyway, even if there *are* guards they can't hear us.'

'No, my Lord, neither can your father. To speak to your father, you must dismount and become visible, both to him and his enemies. Come, we will not take long.'

Bud swung away, melting smoothly through the wall opposite into yet another corridor. Jack sat silently, letting the camel go where he wanted, feeling almost as impatient as Saleem. He patted the woolly neck affectionately. *Got more brains than all of us put together*, he told himself.

'There is no one, my Lord.' Bud turned and, retracing his steps, entered the cell.

In a flash, Saleem was off his back. '*Farver!*' he gasped. 'You're alive! We've been searching everywhere.'

The man lifted his head from his writing, rubbing his eyes as if unable to believe in the mirage. Saleem knelt down and hugged him.

'*Saleem!* How did you get in here? The door is firmly bolted and there is no window. Am I imagining it?'

'No, it's really me. Here, pinch me.'

Prince Salah clutched his son's hand. 'It *is* a miracle but I do not understand?'

He glanced wildly round the cell, his eyes coming to rest on Bud's neck and head. He studied him silently then passed on more slowly to Jack, who'd emerged from nowhere and appeared to be nonchalantly sliding down the face of the wall.

'Jacob!' he said, smiling faintly. 'The inestimable Jacob. So he has not let me down. That explains it.' Prince Salah straightened his bowed shoulders. 'And who are you, young man? You seem very young to be in the rescue business.'

'My name's Jack Burnside, sir. But I didn't actually come here to rescue you, I came to find Saleem. He's a mate. And I found Mercedes.'

The man looked puzzled. 'Enterprising, though somewhat confusing, I fear, for a man who has had little to eat today. However, I am sure all will be revealed if I ask the right questions. No doubt you are one of Jacob's prodigies?'

'I don't know the meaning of prodigy, sir, but I have a little food here, if you're interested.'

'Good on you, Jack, I forgot,' muttered Saleem ashamed.

'It's okay, Saleem, I didn't particularly bring it for your father. I thought I might need it myself after all this searching. Here, sir.'

The man smiled, thanking Jack for the pieces of bread and meat he had thoughtfully wrapped in a paper napkin, remembering how hungry Saleem had been. They watched in silence, as the half-starved man ate the pieces rapidly, almost gulping them down.

'I'm sorry it wasn't very much, sir.'

'For me it was ambrosia, if you know what that is?'

Jack shook his head.

Prince Salah smiled slightly and waved his hand. 'Never mind. And you, beast, I gather Jacob is not with you. Why not?'

'My master has as yet no means to enter the palace. All the secret ways are guarded and every armed man, for miles, is already here in the dungeons,' Bud admitted, somewhat reluctantly.

Just for a second Prince Salah looked very weary, passing his hand across his eyes. 'Then I have to wait longer.'

'Only a little longer, my Lord. My accurs-ed master, being unable to come himself, sent this young infidel,' the camel said eagerly.

A fleeting smile passed across the Prince's face. 'I am ashamed to admit my incarceration has left my wits weak from lack of food, so that I do not understand. Surely, Jacob could have availed himself of your services? Walls hold no barrier for you. Why involve strangers?'

'Actually, Bud, that's the bit I don't understand,' admitted Jack.

'Huh! About that I am not surprised, for the ways of my master are of a higher plain than mere mortals, such as yourself, infidel,' rebuked the camel.

The Prince raised his eyebrows, frowning. 'Do not think you are going to avoid my questions by insulting this young man. He sounds extremely enterprising, from what little I have gleaned of the situation. He has found Saleem and Mercedes, although why Mercedes is lost I have yet to discover. So tell me, camel, and I will judge.'

'When the box was stolen ...'

'*Jacob's box?*' said the Prince sharply.

Bud's harness jingled as he nodded. 'When the box was stolen by your curs-ed brother, the Prince Saladin ...'

'Ah yes, my brother,' said Prince Salah sadly. 'I do not know how I could have possessed such a brother. Continue camel.'

Bud glared at being interrupted. 'When the box was stolen by your curs-ed brother, the Prince Saladin, my master first sent word to his daughter, Mercedes, to search for it ...'

'You mean, she was kept here? She was not allowed to leave?'

'No, my Lord Prince. After the coup no one was allowed to leave.' Bud shook his head, the bells on his harness ringing merrily, quite out of place in the grim starkness of the prison. 'Without fighting men,' he continued, 'my master knew he would need to seek out an army from another world, an army that has no need for gates or pathways. With such a task to undertake, he could not also come to the palace.'

'I see,' said Prince Salah thoughtfully. He turned to his son. 'For how long have you been a prisoner, Saleem?'

'Momfs now.'

'Ah, you are so thin I should have guessed.'

'As for being thin, Farver, it's you who's thin; you're half-starved. With Jack here, I can eat whenever I want.'

Bud spat. '*Pfliipft!*'

Jack turned to look at the camel who, offended at his story being interrupted yet again, had withdrawn into the wall.

'Continue, Bud, but for goodness sake stop being such a wus,' he said sternly.

83

'Wus, infidel! What is this wus?'

'Nana, idiot, lame-brain, anything you like. Temperamental would fit right in here.'

'Huh, and do I start yet again from the words, *without the box ...*'

'NO!' pleaded Saleem and Jack together.

Bud glared angrily, raising his upper lip to expose his gums and long, yellow teeth. 'It was then my master had a most brilliant idea. The Prince Saladin has a passion for the game of football,' he continued, his voice still sounding sulky, like a six-year old who's just had his chocolate bar confiscated. 'I travelled many moons in a paper parcel, to bring back the most famous of footballers. He would teach the boys of the palace to play good football by day – and seek out knowledge of you and your son, my Lord, by night – *may Saladin be curs-ed for what he has done to you.*'

The Prince, still holding his son, smiled faintly. 'Jacob is nothing if not ...'

'Tricky,' suggested Bud hopefully.

'Actually, I was going to say resourceful. And are you the famous footballer?'

'Well, no, not exactly,' admitted Jack with a grin.

'No, I didn't think so. So the plan went wrong?'

Bud looked aggrieved. 'It went wrong, my Lord, though not from any fault of my own. However,' he added more cheerfully, 'this plan is definitely better.'

Prince Salah smiled. 'From that hurried endorsement, I gather you are getting away with it?'

'Yes, sir, thanks to Jacob's magic. And Saleem is let out of his prison long enough to help at the training sessions. As you know, the match is in a few days.'

'Of course, the football match in Tigrit, I had forgotten.'

'Not Tigrit, Farver,' interrupted Saleem, 'right here. Saladin has built a stadium outside the walls. That's why he needed a footballer — to coach his team.'

'Except we've only got ten in the team,' said Jack.

'Ten?' exclaimed Prince Salah.

Jack nodded. 'I don't mind playing but what happens if someone is injured, we don't have any reserves.'

'Saleem?'

His son shrugged. 'They're the only servant boys left in the palace. Saladin's locked up so many people, the rest have run away.'

Prince Salah shook his head sadly. 'How could one man become so wicked — and he my brother.'

'Tomorrow night, sir, Bud — that's what I call my camel — we will ride back to Jacob and tell him we've found you.' Jack glanced down at his watch, the dial ominously pointing towards four. 'Sir, we got to go now, *at once*, we've stayed far too long.'

Saleem jumped to his feet, stamping his foot angrily. 'Jack, we can't go wivout my farver,' he protested. 'We can't leave him here.'

'We have to, Saleem. He's chained to the wall. Anyway, judging by my past efforts, even if we managed to free your father he wouldn't come with us. It seems,' added Jack bitterly, 'as if everyone's having such a good time that *nothing, but nothing*, will get them to leave.'

'You are quite right, young man. I cannot leave without my men and, to do that, you must find the box.'

'But sir, I don't understand how finding a small box is more important than rescuing you and Saleem?'

'The box contains an immense power, Jack. With it, we will all be free. Without it …' A black shadow seemed to cross the Prince's sight and he shivered. 'So search hard, Jack. When it is found, do not delay for anything, take it to Jacob. You must promise me this, Jack. *The moment you find it …*'

Jack studied the haggard figure chained to the wall. There was so much here he didn't understand, so much Jacob had never told him, but if getting the Prince free meant he had to find the box then, with Bud's help, he'd turn the palace upside down if necessary.

He nodded. 'Yes, sir, I promise I'll find the box and take it to Jacob.'

The Prince raised his hand and smiled slightly. 'I will wait eagerly for your return. Go in peace, Jack Burnside.'

'But Jack, Farver needs some more food. It won't take a minute.'

Jack glanced at his watch again and shook his head. 'There's no time. I've got to get you back to your cell.'

'But … '

'Go on, Saleem, *I order it.*' It was the ruler speaking.

Saleem stiffened to attention, as a soldier under command would do. 'Yes sir,' he said. Crossing the floor he clasped Jack's hand to help him mount. 'Be patient, Farver, we'll be back and with the real cavalry.'

Chapter Ten

The Thief from the Sky

His shackled feet were too heavy to lift off the ground. He tried again and again but couldn't move them. The guards were laughing, prodding him with their spears.

'No!' he shouted out as the cell door slammed shut leaving him in the dark, the noise vibrating throughout his head. Claaa … ng! Then again, even louder, Claaa … ng! The dark was overpowering, like thick globules of tar, and he couldn't see. Sweat poured down his face as he tried to force his eyes open. How had they caught him? They hadn't been seen he'd have known. They couldn't have been seen; it was a mistake!

'It's a mistake,' he yelled.

Thump! There it was again. *Thump!*

With a shockwave running through him, Jack woke up. Someone was banging on his door and it was broad daylight. He jumped out of bed running across the room to open it. It was the servant with his breakfast. He rubbed his eyes feeling absolutely shattered but grateful it had only been a dream, even if it was scary.

The servant crossed to the balcony pointing at the sun. 'Yella! Yella!'

Jack looked at him and then at the sun puzzled. The man pointed at the sun again and pantomimed someone kicking a ball. Jack glanced at his watch. *Rats!* He'd overslept. 'Shrukran,' he shouted, heading for the bathroom.

The servant grinned at him, collected his clothes for washing, and left the room, closing the door behind him.

Jack turned on the shower and stood under it, trying to clear his head. He felt rotten, not a bit like eating. Quite the reverse. Right now he felt like throwing-up, the ugly dream still haunting him. The cold water blasted down on his eyes, screwed up tightly against the light. Gradually his sickness lessened as the menacing dream faded.

'Right,' he shouted. Leaping out of the water he quickly dried himself. 'From now on I'll concentrate on football and leave the other stuff to Jacob. As of tonight he can take charge.'

Hungrily, he cut some cheese and, plastering it onto bread, added some honey. He ate frantically now but long before he'd cleared his plate, a thunderous knocking heralded his guide to the football stadium.

The early morning sun shone in the clear blue sky, a solitary bird cruising overhead like it had each day; everything by now so familiar that Jack felt he could have been doing it all his life. If only they had eleven extra men to play a proper game. He glanced across at the stand. Even Saladin looked more relaxed, chatting to his courtiers.

There were several veiled women watching and, although he didn't want to be seen checking them out too closely, Jack was sure one of them was Mercedes.

I wish she'd had the sense to stay away, he thought, as he organised the teams for the five-a-side – goal, two defensive players and two in midfield. He called out, 'Iqbal and Ahmed in goal,' hoping he'd got the names right. 'Ali, tell Hassan he can take goal in the second game.'

'OK! Jack,' said Saleem, keeping his eyes on the ground.

Jack glanced at him, knowing his friend felt as tired as he did. Even so, he hadn't looked at Jack once, which pretty much confirmed it *was* Mercedes in the stand. Saleem was too scared to look up in case she gave them away.

He blew his whistle for the kick off. He'd called his teams Hurricanes and Tornadoes, words the boys could easily pronounce. It was the Tornadoes who took possession of the ball with Farouk, one of the defenders, immediately racing up the wing and stealing the ball from his own team. The boy continued up the pitch, leaving the two midfielders wandering around behind him, wondering where the ball had gone.

Jack watched closely, storing up all the problems to sort out later. Fortunately today, Iqbal in goal decided to stay put, contenting himself with shouting orders. Jack sprinted up the pitch just as Farouk was tackled by one of the midfielders, who kicked him in the shins. Jack quickly stopped the game, beckoning to Saleem.

'Er ... Ali, what's his name?' he asked.

'Majuud.'

'Well, please tell Majuud he can't tackle by kicking his opponent in the shins.'

Saleem broke into a torrent of Arabic which made Majuud grin.

'OK!' He put his thumb up at Jack.

'Oh, and while you're at it, tell Farouk he has two midfielders in his team, and they'd like a chance to kick the ball.'

He awarded a free kick to the Tornadoes and, seconds later, Omar, one of the midfielders, finally got into the game and, taking the pass from Farouk, quickly sent it on to his team-mate.

Jack grimaced as he watched them race up to the ball – stop dead – look around – then kick. He let it go hoping, by the time the match came, they might have learned how pass the ball on the run.

Yard by yard, the two midfielders worked their way towards the goal, constantly frustrated by one of the defenders who, darting from side to side, blocked them. Jack watched the young boy dodging about, his arms akimbo. He might be little but he was like greased lightning. Finally, Omar tapped the ball neatly through the defender's legs. He stopped, his foot poised to make the shot, and looked down. It was enough. The little defender twisted on his heel. Doubling-back, he deflected the shot with his head and then, with incredible cheek, took the ball.

The youngster flew down the pitch, before reluctantly passing to Majuud, as the two midfielders from the Tornadoes charged. Changing direction, they tore after Majuud. For a second, Majuud stood there as if turned to stone then, losing his head completely, kicked out wildly. The ball skimmed over the turf and dribbled over the sidelines with the little defender diving after it. Hooking it in with his foot, he continued down the pitch, Omar and the other boys storming after him. A minute later he scored for the Hurricanes. The jubilant team rushed headlong into a huddle of backslapping, the goal-scorer hidden somewhere in the middle, as Jack blew his whistle to disallow the goal.

'OK! Break it up,' he shouted to Saleem, heading towards the huddle.

The noise level rose – everyone having something to say – with the five boys, from the Tornadoes team, not slow to join in. Jack gave his whistle an extra sharp blast, hoping Saladin and his courtiers were too busy gossiping to notice the loss of discipline.

'For goodness sake, Saleem, *get them sorted*,' he shouted, only realising what he'd said by Saleem's look of horror. For one heart-stopping moment Jack thought he'd blown it. He glanced furtively across at the stand. Saladin had his back-turned and was busily chatting. Jack blew a long blast on his whistle and dived into the melee to hide his burning face, furious with himself for being so stupid.

Overhead the bird spiralled lazily as it had done since dawn. Now, ceasing its languid flight, it dived towards the ground. As yet no one had noticed it, Jack too busy trying to restore order, while the spectators, absorbed in their gossiping, were enjoying some free entertainment. Seconds later, a thunderous sound of flapping wings, as if some prehistoric beast was launching an attack, stopped the row on the pitch – DEAD – the arguments cut off in mid-sentence.

The boys stood there like statues, their faces upturned towards the rushing noise of the bird's flight. The bird accelerated, diving faster and faster, the sound reverberating off the galvanised roof of the stand to a deafening pitch. High in the sky it had been a black speck. Now, as it drew near the ground, it began to resemble a ferocious ostrich. Its beak outstretched and agape, it swooped on the rucksack lying unattended on the bench. It pulled at its straps lifting it and, in less than a second, was flapping away.

Jack felt rather than saw what happened, as if the rucksack had been on his back and had come alive. He let out a bloodcurdling yell pointing to the bird.

'ST-OP IT!'

No one moved; the boys on the pitch, their feet rooted to the earth like saplings, their mouths open with astonishment. They gazed after the retreating bird, its size and weight making it difficult to gain height.

Jack ran towards it, his arms waving madly. *'Stop it. Someone stop it!'* Saladin shouted. Then there were men running in all directions. The women cowered back in the stand, uttering a sort of high-pitched wailing noise, terrified the bird was going to attack them.

Jack changed direction, running towards Saladin.

'Sir,' he gasped. 'The bird has my rucksack and B ...' He stopped abruptly, his hand half-flying to his mouth in panic at what he'd nearly said. 'It has my game plan in it,' he hastily improvised. 'I did it last night.'

'Wait!'

Jack waited, half-turning to watch as guards burst out of the watch towers and spread out along the ramparts, their bows at the ready. Arrows flew into the air – a deadly black rain – aimed at the bird slowly flapping past them.

Jack found himself muttering, *'please – please – please'*, his fingers tightly crossed behind his back, hardly bearing to look.

There was silence, broken only by the hiss of arrows. Several hit the rucksack. There came a shout of triumph as an arrow reached its target, its tip tearing through the black feathers to pierce the bird's soft underbelly. The bird squawked in pain, staggered slightly and flew on, the arrow still embedded in its body. Gradually, the rushing noise died away as its great wings lifted it out of reach. *Then, there was nothing.*

Jack felt sick. Bud was gone! What was he going to do? How would he get home now?

'You may continue your game.'

The silken voice jolted him back into wakefulness.

'It was after all only a bag. A bag is of little importance and I dismiss such a trivial incident. However, since you are our honoured guest, I have instructed guards to go after the bird. The bag will be found and brought back to you. Continue.'

Saladin clapped his hands for silence. His courtiers waited obediently for the ruler to begin a conversation, before breaking out once again into their noisy gossiping – the sole topic of conversation, the terrifying incident that had just taken place.

'Thank you, sir,' said Jack slowly and bowed. Realising what he'd done, he turned and walked shakily back down the steps, trying hard not to kick himself.

'Bloody hell fire!' he muttered furiously under his breath. *Fancy bowing to the bloke like that.* Talk about a dead give-away. Now Saladin has to know there's something real important in my bag. What a mess!' He looked across to the middle of the pitch where Saleem stood, gazing dejectedly after the retreating bird. At least he had no need to explain it to Saleem.

Gritting his teeth, he blew his whistle to start the game again, the little team instantly in action, forgetting the drama in the excitement of the game, only Saleem getting slowly to his feet.

'Come on, Ali,' Jack shouted a warning. 'We've got a game to win.'

He finished the session, trying to put on a good show and throw

Saladin off the scent, watching anxiously as guards approached the stand. There was some conversation. They turned and walked away.

At the end of the game, the man who acted as Saladin's armrest beckoned to him. Nervously, Jack approached the ruler. Snake eyes bored into him as if searching out his soul.

'You seemed to be very distraught at the loss of your bag. Surely it is not of such great value. With one of these,' Saladin pointed to a ruby, one of several embellishing the embroidery on the front of his tunic, 'you could buy several thousand.'

Jack stared at the ruby, which glowed like a burning red fire. Saleem had explained that Saladin was far too mean to buy more than one ceremonial outfit, which the servant boys took turns in wearing. He could see why, the ruby alone had to have cost a fortune.

He swallowed loudly. 'I don't like losing things, sir,' he said. 'I can write out the game plan again, but I carry personal things in my rucksack which I'd hate to lose.'

'*Such as?*' The words slid out of the ruler's mouth.

Jack glanced at Saladin, now leaning forward in his seat to stare at him, his voice a mere whisper. He forced himself to look the man in the eye, a bland and innocent expression sweeping across his face.

'My football gear, of course, and my spare trainers. Oh, and I carry something my father made for me when I was a kid – a wooden camel. Never go anywhere without it. No, the real loss is my number 7 shirt. It's brand new and I'd hate to lose it.'

'Aaaah!'

Jack suppressed a shudder, continuing to try and look as if there were nothing in the world more important than his shirt.

'Was it an accident?' he said, breaking the silence.

'Why do you ask that?'

'Well, could the bird have been spying?' The words were out before Jack could stop them.

Quick as a flash, the honey-tongued voice came back at him. 'How curious you should say that? A bird spying?' Saladin hissed. 'And what reason would you have for thinking such a thing?'

'I don't know,' Jack shrugged nonchalantly, his mind working overtime, trying to undo the damage. 'Stupid when you come to think about it. I guess I've been watching too much television ... only, I've never seen a bird as large as that. We don't have anything half that size in England.'

He shrugged again, trying to buy time and find words that wouldn't get him into yet more trouble.

'*But a bag*! It's such a funny thing for a bird to steal. I could understand if there was food in it. But it just went for the bag, and the only person who has anything to gain from stealing it ...' his voice tailed off, 'is your neighbour, Sheikh Mendorun,' he ended lamely.

Unwillingly, he forced himself to look up. Saladin was watching him closely, unblinking. Silence, while the ruler continued to study him.

'We will continue to search for your bag. If it is to be found, we will find it. However, my men report that the bird has reached the mountains. In that case,' Saladin paused. 'As I said, it is of small importance.'

He said nothing more, simply gesturing with his hand to let Jack know his audience was over.

A minute later the ground was deserted; Saleem marched back to prison, his team disappeared through the gate and Saladin – with his retainers – once more inside the palace.

Jack sat a moment longer, before clattering down into the locker room to change back into his white tunic. He kicked at the wooden benches in anger. Saladin wasn't thick, he might not have heard Jack call Saleem by name, but he'd certainly picked up on his anxiety about losing his bag. And why on earth would anyone think of a bird spying, unless they knew something Saladin didn't?

Slowly, he climbed back up the steps and, leaving the stand, made his way round the boundary. And what had Saladin told him about Mendorun? *Nothing – absolutely nothing – not even the guy's name!*

His legs felt like wool and he couldn't have run even if the bird were after him. He gazed miserably across the ground, trying to stop tears welling up. His nightmare had just come true. Now he was a prisoner.

* * *

Dinner, served in the yellow room, was as good as it had been the night before, but although Jack ate, he didn't pay much attention to the food.

Neither Saladin nor his retainers had been at training that evening, only the man whom Saladin had used as an interpreter. Thinking the Prince was late, the boys had waited; Saleem on the ground in the middle of his guards, Jack on the bench with the team huddled in a circle next to him. Finally, after half-an-hour, he asked if the ruler was going to come and watch. The man shrugged.

'Do we start training or wait?' Jack said.

'Start now,' the man nodded.

Taking this to be a 'yes', Jack began a warm up, keeping an eye on the gate throughout the hour-long session, in case Saladin did appear. But it had been difficult to concentrate. Every time he looked up, there was the empty stand where Saladin usually sat intently watching the game. Where was he? Where had he gone? Gradually a nagging suspicion, that the ruler had gone to make enquiries about him, took hold and failed to disappear.

Jack kept his eyes on his plate, hoping to pick up some sort of clue as to Saladin's state of mind. Was he suspicious? It was impossible to tell.

Saladin, seated opposite, looked anything but suspicious as he chewed and burped his way through a colossal amount of food. Still, he hadn't uttered a word.

All at once, Saladin gave an ear-piercing belch. 'Your bag has been returned, Mr Burnside.'

Jack gave a silent cheer. 'Oh, that's great, sir,' he said aloud. 'Thank you. Where was it found?'

'I paid a visit to my neighbour, Sheikh Mendorun. I explained to him that you were my guest and asked for his help in finding the bag.'

Jack blinked. 'Er … um … But you shouldn't have gone to all that trouble.'

'It was no trouble, Mr Burnside. I had matters I wished to discuss with the Sheikh.' Saladin waved his hand, dismissing the incident.

'I'm very grateful. Now I can wear my shirt for the game.'

'Aaaah, yes, your shirt. Naturally.' The velvet-tongued words slipped out of the fleshy mouth making Jack's flesh crawl.

Saladin clapped his hands and a servant appeared carrying the rucksack. It was Omar, obviously his turn in the gold robe and turban. He grinned at Jack, offering him the bag.

When he saw it, Jack felt an irresistible urge to grab it and run. He forced himself to sit still, letting Omar place the bag on the seat beside him, hoping Saladin wouldn't notice that his hands were shaking. He looked down, spotting the jagged tear in the fabric where an arrow had pierced it.

'Your possession's are intact, Mr Burnside?'

'I was going to leave it till we'd finished our meal, sir, but if you wish I'll check now,' Jack said.

He quickly ran his hands round the inside of the bag, identifying objects by touch: his shirt – shorts – book – socks – sock pads – trainers – notebook. He swept them aside, feeling everywhere, panic rising in him as he peered into the bag.

'There is something wrong, Mr Burnside?'

Not daring to look up in case his eyes betrayed him, Jack forced himself to reply, 'No, sir. Everything seems okay, except the toy animal my father gave me. But my *shirt* is here.'

'Of course, your wooden animal! How tiresome. Even had I known, I could not have asked the Sheikh about it. It would not have been polite to question one's host. One can hardly suggest that someone has stolen something from the bag.'

'Not stolen, sir. Perhaps it dropped out.'

'I think that would be most likely, Mr Burnside. But as you yourself said, it has no value.'

I didn't say that! Jack bit his tongue to stop himself blurting out the words. Saladin was playing him like a cat played with a mouse. Was it possible that Sheikh Mendorun had found Bud and realised what powers the statue possessed? In that case Bud was gone for good and he had a serious problem.

Feeling hollow inside Jack got slowly to his feet, grasping his ruck sack tightly against his chest, as Saladin called for his armrest. Silently, he waited while the ruler made his ponderous way out of the yellow tent, after courteously wishing his guest a good night's sleep.

Outside, the night was dark. A wind had got up, sweeping thick black clouds of rain across the landscape. Lights were burning in the courtyard, rainwater trickling gently through the branches of the palm trees. Jack, gazing down from his balcony, thought how peaceful the gardens seemed. Tomorrow, he'd ask Saladin if he could sit there. But for now, there was nothing he could do except sleep.

He yawned, suddenly very tired. It had been a terrible day; hopefully tomorrow would be better. In any case, there really was no need to panic. In a few days it was the match, when Jacob had said he would fetch him. But what about his promise to Prince Salah; to find the box and take it to Jacob? Jack shook his head sadly. There was nothing he could do about that. Without Bud, there was nothing he could do about anything.

He climbed wearily into bed, still trying to work out if Bud's disappearance put him in danger. Instead, his mind wandered off on a track all on its own, strange thoughts popping in and out until, exhausted, he fell asleep.

Chapter Eleven

Honey Cakes

The football pitch resembled a battleground with guards everywhere; guards patrolling the battlements, guards round the perimeter of the ground and flanking the stand, where Saladin and his retainers lounged. And they weren't there to boost crowd numbers, they were heavily armed. Those on the ramparts with spears or bows and arrows; those on the ground with swords – curved swords – their edges so sharp they glinted, their metal surface so brilliant, the sun's reflection in them dazzled the eyes.

Yet here the similarity to a war zone ended. Out on the pitch, completely oblivious of the armed men, a match was being played. It might well have been a cup final for the enthusiasm displayed by its ten participants and their audience. Of course it was only five-a-side, on a shortened pitch, and only for thirty minutes, but it was still a match. In Sudana where matches were a rare event, this was an exciting one.

A great cheer rose into the air, as Iqbal, in goal, proved himself quite brilliant, blocking a really good header from Majuud. Their audience, needing no encouragement, had instantly taken sides picking their favourites. Jack, glancing across at the stand, saw coins passing between them as they backed a team or a player. Applauding or groaning at the right moment, they created so much noise the sentries, constantly forgot their duty to watch the skies and joined in. Even Saladin talked and laughed like any normal man.

Jack had slept badly, constantly waking to check if Bud had returned, and he got up feeling as if his head and feet were filled with lead. All he wanted to do was stay in his room but he couldn't, everyone's safety depended on him keeping up the pretence that he was the great Jack Burnside.

When Saleem appeared, his footsteps dogged as always by his faithful shadows, he had caught Jack's eye, and raised his eyebrows asking the question, *'Is Bud back?'* It didn't take a genius to work out that Saleem would be feeling far worse than him, once again locked in a cell with no means of escape, and no way to let his father know. The crowd booed and, catching the tail end of an illegal tackle, Jack hastily blew his whistle, trying to get up to speed with the game. He watched carefully as Hassan took the free kick. Then, glancing at his watch, blew the final whistle. The crowd cheered the Hurricanes, who had won the game three-two.

Saladin beckoned and Jack ran up.

'An excellent game, most exciting.'

'Thank you, sir. Your team's great. I wish I'd a month to train them, not just a few days.'

He wriggled uncomfortably, feeling eyes on the back of his neck. Flashing a glance over his shoulder, he glimpsed one of the women staring fixedly at him. Thank goodness it was only one of the women. He relaxed and looked away, concentrating on Saladin.

'I have some gifts for you.' The ruler waved his hand languidly in the direction of a large package.

'Thank you, sir. What is it?' Jack stepped across to the package, once again aware of eyes boring into his back.

'Open it.' The soft tones of Saladin's voice came sliding out of his monstrous frame, like a spider stalking its prey. So sickly sweet was his voice, Jack decided that of the two options – friendly or suspicious – friendly was the worst.

He opened it up. Inside were the shirts he'd asked for; white, with black numbers on their backs, and black shorts.

'That's great, sir,' he exclaimed, genuinely pleased. 'That'll make all the difference.'

'I am glad you are pleased, Mr Burnside. It gives me great pleasure to please a guest, such as yourself.'

Jack ears felt as if they were about to burst into flame. Casually, he looked up into the stand where the women sat, their faces covered by the long black burqa, which they wore outside the harem. He looked along the line of chattering, laughing women, meeting the eyes boring into him. *Mercedes!*

The brown eyes flashed momentarily, only this time he caught the slight movement of her right shoulder. *Saladin! What about Saladin?* He lifted up one of the shirts and held it against him for size. *Mercedes was trying to tell him something about Saladin, but what?*

'Right size, too, sir. I'm sure all the boys will play better with these. Do you want them used for their next practice?'

Saladin casually clapped his hands, holding his right arm in the air.

'I think, Mr Burnside,' he said, as a retainer rushed up with a small box of sweetmeats. 'I think, Mr Burnside, the team could wear their shirts and shorts in the morning – shall we say, as a dress rehearsal.'

The retainer flipped open the lid of the casket. Saladin paused, the fingers of both hands hovering, obviously undecided which to choose. He delicately abstracted a honey cake between his thumb and first two fingers and looked at it gloatingly.

'A sweet, Mr Burnside,' he said, stuffing the cake into his mouth.

He nodded to the retainer, who moved to Jack's side. The little cakes were like those Jack had eaten at Jacob's, a mixture of honey and nuts wrapped in a flaky pastry, but about half the size – a perfect size to fit into the mouth.

'Thank you, sir,' said Jack and stretched out his hand. A current of electricity surged through it and he jumped violently, his hand flying forward of its own accord – as if it were alive.

Instantly, Saladin sat up, staring fixedly at Jack. 'There is something the matter?'

'No, sir,' Jack replied, thinking fast. He held up his hand and shook it. 'Cramp. That's all.' He smiled innocently.

His hand moved again, drawn forcibly towards the tiny jewelled casket as if it contained a magnet. Quickly, he dipped his fingers in, pulling out one of the little cakes.

'I love these, sir. Wish I could eat them always.'

Saladin waved his hand impatiently at the servant. He said something in Arabic and the man bowed, leaving the small box by Saladin's side.

'Sit down, Mr Burnside, and take another, and while you are eating you can tell me how you are choosing the team.'

Jack tucked his right hand under his arm, sitting on his left. 'Well, sir ... No, thank you, I won't have another. Um ... Well – er – Hassan is definitely going to be in goal. He's really good and, with training, you'll have a real star goalkeeper.'

'How very gratifying.' Saladin bowed slightly.

'There's two others – Iqbal and Yusef – they're pretty good, too. They will be my centre defence, because they're bigger than the other boys. Then Omar, the eldest of the boys – if you remember he scored a goal today – he'll play centre midfield, with Majuud on the left wing. And I want to play Yazim on the right wing. He might be small but he's fast and can run rings round the others. He's so fast, I thought I'd give him a chance to score some goals.'

'Right wing! I understand that is your position, Mr Burnside.'

'Yes, sir, I'm happiest in midfield, but I can play anywhere – except in goal – and I have practised all sorts of formations, as you've seen.'

'We have not yet seen you play. Have a sweet.'

Jack's hand flew out from under his arm, straight to the box. He tried not to think about it, simply taking a sweet and concentrating on the heavenly taste of warm honey and nuts.

'It'll be fun, sir,' he said, through a mouthful of juice.

The ruler closed the jewelled box and stood up. 'I hope you have a pleasant afternoon, Mr Burnside.'

He beckoned to his retainers and his palanquin appeared. Jack, still munching, stood up, wrapping his arms round one another to stop them moving.

Within a few minutes, the ruler and his entourage had left the stand. Jack watched the jewelled casket closely as it lay on the folds of Saladin's monstrous stomach. Miserably, he picked up the case of gear and made his way down to the locker room. They might have found the box but without Bud, there wasn't a damn thing they could do about it.

Chapter Twelve

The Monster Crow

Jack woke suddenly. He lay there feeling drowsy and disorientated, wondering if he'd missed out on dinner. He remembered coming in from evening training and guessed he must have fallen asleep. Bleary-eyed, he gazed over towards the open window, expecting to see stars already lighting the sky. Instead, the air was densely black as if the sky had been draped in a cloak, and there was an eerie silence – like someone holding his breath. Was it going to rain again? He hoped not. It had poured the night before and had been so cold, he'd been glad of an extra cover on his bed.

A scratching, rather like long nails tapping on a door, broke the silence. Jack listened, barbs of goose flesh breaking out on his body as he watched the heavy blackness of the air change shape, closing in on the bed. Too late he realised what was about to happen.

He dived for the lamp as claws struck at his chest and a rasping beak laid open his finger. He beat at them with his fist and kicked out, his legs meeting air. There was a sudden rush of wind in his face. He flinched back against the pillow, his arm protecting his eyes. Now, he could sense the force trying to remove him bodily from his bed but he was powerless, stranded on his back, the claws of his attacker welded to his tunic. Jack pummelled the claws again and again, kicking out wildly, all the time shuffling towards the bedside lamp. Half-turning he reached over, crying out as sharp nails pierced the thin cotton of his tunic, tearing away skin on his back.

Next second, he was being dragged back across the bed, his fingers still fumbling in the air, no longer in control of his body, as floppy and insubstantial as a rag doll. He gripped the thick cotton of his mattress with both hands but it lifted and buckled like cardboard, moving under him. Panic stricken, he grabbed the iron frame of his bed and held on. Instantly, the legs of the bed lifted into the air, jerking over the uneven surface of the floor.

There were no thoughts now in Jack's head other than survival. Loosing his hold on the bed frame, he grabbed his pillow and scuttled down the bed towards his attacker. He swung it against the claws gripping him, anger taking over from fear. He felt them slacken and, without stopping to think, swung his legs up, his head and shoulders buried in the mattress. Slamming his feet against the wall, he exploded upwards, with all the power in the trained muscles of his legs, and felt his feet ram something soft and downy, knocking it off balance. The force of his kick had thrown him forwards on to his knees. Now, using the mattress as a springboard, he rolled straight back onto his shoulders, tucked his knees into his chest and jack-knifed his body, double kicking into a wall of feathers.

He was free. He flung himself across the bed and, twisting back onto his knees, stretched out his arm towards the lamp. His fingers caught the knob.

'TURN – TURN – FOR GOD'S SAKE!'

There was a flash of light.

'HELP!' he screamed. 'HELP, SOMEONE HELP. I'M BEING ATTACKED.' The light from his lamp cast its shadow on to the wall. A shadow which kicked and bucked, the camel's teeth and feet reaching out even before it was fully-formed to strike at the feathers of the monstrous bird.

'BUD, it's you!' Jack fell back on his bed sobbing and out of breath, his fingers bleeding onto the quilted cover as he pulled it over his head for protection.

The room was full of fear and anger. Jack could sense it wafting out from the bird, beating its wings against the flank of the camel in an attempt to avoid the lashing teeth. Then it was over. Jack heard the crack as the camel swung the neck of the bird against the wall. It fell limply to the ground, blood oozing from the wound on its back, its neck lolling awkwardly to one side, its black wings spread out.

'*Take that*, you carrion of the Nile, you worm of the Sahara.'

Jack peeped over the bedcover gripped against his head. He hiccupped and laughed shakily.

'Is it dead?' he said. He leapt out of bed and rushed to hug the camel. 'Oh, Bud, *it's great to see you,*' and kissed him on his nose.

Bud blinked with surprise. 'Huh, I think it would be more to the point if you offered praises to the Gods, for it is they who should be thanked for my safe arrival. Still, it is encouraging to know that the infidel is pleased to see me.'

'And how! Bud, you've no idea!' Jack looked down at the monster bird on the floor. 'Whatever is it?'

'A crow, curse its black wings.'

'It can't be. It's huge! What on earth's going on?'

'I believe, my Lord, that someone is trying to stop you playing the match.'

'But who? Surely you don't mean Saladin, so ... who? Mendorun?'

The camel nodded.

'But that's crazy? Nobody does that over a little game of football,' Jack said indignantly. He was silent a moment before adding, 'Does that mean he might try again?'

'Very possibly, my Lord. You will need to take great care.'

Jack shivered, suddenly aware if Bud hadn't turned up, he would now be dead or flying over the mountains, caught in those gigantic talons.

'You arrived in the nick of time, Bud. I thought you were lost.'

There was a noise of spitting. '*Pfliipft!* I nearly was,' came the mournful reply.

'Tell me.'

'Well, I would, except that you are succeeding in depriving me of air, which is essential if I am to breathe.'

Jack grinned, for the first time in two days. 'Sorry, Bud, tell away.'

'I suffered a terrible shock being lifted into the air by that wretched bird and an even worse one, when an arrow penetrated the cloth of the bag,' began the camel.

'Yeah! Yeah! As a matter of fact so did I,' Jack said sternly, rapidly recovering from his ordeal. 'My lifeline back home, remember.'

'Complaints, complaints, but what else would you expect of infidels, always thinking of themselves,' grumbled the camel.

'And?'

'The bird flew high above the mountains, heading towards Mendorun's kingdom. I knew there would be danger if I was seen by Mendorun, for he is clever enough to know that I am a very *extraordinary* camel,' said Bud, his tone haughty. 'But I have few powers as a statue. As we passed over some water, the bird flew lower and lower. Did an arrow strike the bird?'

Jack nodded.

'So that is why. It was injured. I could feel the bag brushing the surface of the water, so I chewed through the bag and dropped out.'

'You chewed through the bag?'

'That is what I said.'

'How could you chew through the bag, you were a wooden statue.'

'All right then, I dropped out, *satisfied*.'

Jack grinned. 'So you dropped out into the water?'

'No! *I dropped into some bushes at the side of the lake*.' Bud glared. 'Christian, if you are going to quibble about everything I tell you, I will not tell you.'

Bud's tone was so dignified that Jack laughed. 'Then what?'

'It rained,' said Bud gloomily.

'But you said darkness was your home.'

'Once I am formed, infidel, but without light I cannot manifest myself. Tonight there was moonlight and so …'

Bud didn't finish what he was saying. He stopped in mid-sentence as running footsteps approached down the corridor.

'Bud, disappear quickly,' Jack whispered as they reached his door. It banged open, crashing against the wall behind and two guards, spears preceding them, ran in shouting.

Jack might not have understood their language but he understood their alarm. They glanced round the room, not missing anything from the bloodstained bedcover to the carcass on the ground. Whilst one guarded the door, the other inspected the bird, turning it over with the point of his spear. He said something and both men glanced at Jack now seated at the end of the bed.

'OK!' he said, putting on a grin and giving the thumbs up sign. Surely okay was an international word, whatever language they spoke.

'OK!' replied the guard, flashing him a curious look.

Other noises could now be heard; a soft rustle and silent footsteps, the sort of sound Saladin would make when walking. The two guards froze as the ruler, his arm resting on his bodyguard, appeared.

'Mr Burnside, whatever has been happening? I was on my way to dine when we heard the noise. Allah be praised, you are safe. But you are hurt?'

He turned away, issuing instructions to one of the guards, who ran off to do his bidding, the silken phrases of his voice quite out of place in the blood-spattered room.

'That such an insult should happen to my guest is beyond belief.'

Despite the pain from his wounds Jack listened intently, looking for clues as to Saladin's state of mind. There had been mistrust and suspicion since his bag had been stolen which had scared him.

'Indeed, your youthful frame is deceptively strong to have despatched the bird single-handed,' Saladin added softly, his eyes exploring even the crevices in the walls as if seeking the presence of another person.

Jack held his breath but the face in front of him was bland, showing only concern for his young guest. As far as Saladin was concerned, he was off the hook.

'I was so lucky, sir. I'm pretty strong you know and, with all the football training, I have a kick like a mule. Good job too, it could have been awful.'

'Allah be praised! Now we will talk of more pleasant things. Dinner. It is a particularly fine one this evening. Perhaps you will join me in the green room and we will have music to calm our nerves. If you leave your clothes as they are ...' Saladin wafted his hand vaguely round the room. 'I have already given instructions to prepare for you another chamber. When you return here tomorrow, all of this...' the ruler indicated the carcase and the torn cover, 'will be gone. You have suffered no other hurt?'

'No, sir, only my fingers and the scratches on my back. I'll be there, as soon as I've changed.'

The footsteps disappeared down the corridor and Jack reached wearily for his jeans. If only the night was over. But now Bud was back it was just beginning. As soon as the palace was quiet, they had to break into Saladin's rooms, steal the box and take it to Jacob. He sighed, wishing he could steal Saleem out of his cell instead and head for home on Bud's magic sunbeams. But he couldn't. He'd promised Saleem to get his father free and he couldn't let a mate down, however dangerous it was.

Chapter Thirteen

The Occupant of the Dog Basket

Bud with Jack mounted on his back strode across the courtyard, a pale moon lighting their path through the gardens and entering the women's quarters through a wall. Mercedes was waiting. 'Thought you'd come,' she said.

'How?

'The moonlight, stupid! I knew that wretched beast would be back, unless he met up with a giant woodworm on the way. I tried to tell you at dinner I'd be waitin'.'

Jack smiled to himself, remembering the ferocious glares Mercedes had thrown at him when they met up in the Rainbow Hall. As far as he was concerned, they were like Arabic conversations, they needed an interpreter to be understood.

'Where's Saleem? Nothin's happened, has it?'

Jack shook his head, keeping silent about his tussle with the crow. 'No, I came straight here, the box is more important. Saleem'll understand.'

'I was right, though, wasn't I? Told you the box would find you.'

'*Find me!* It nearly pulled my hand off,' retorted Jack.

'I know,' mocked Mercedes. 'I saw.'

'You saw!' Jack exclaimed, shocked rigid. 'Was it that obvious? Did Saladin see?'

'Even if he did, I bet he just thought you were after another of those yummy cakes.'

'Well, they are good,' he agreed.

'Why do you think I got fat,' laughed Mercedes. 'So, did you find Prince Salah?'

'Of course! You don't *know?*'

'At last, someone with sense! *Of course, I don't know.* All I *know* is that some god-damn monster of a crow stole Bud.'

'Sorry, Mercedes, there's been no time. And I daren't stay now, I've got to get the box to Jacob, and there'll be hell to play when we steal it.'

'No, there won't.'

The girl darted across the room. Pushing aside a table, covered with a brightly coloured carpet, she bent down and prised up a loose tile from the floor. Inside the cavity was a parcel which she handed to Jack.

'What is it?' he said.

'A duplicate box, moron. Pops made it. You don't really think, Saladin isn't goin' to notice when his sweetmeat box suddenly isn't there.'

'Of course I knew,' he retorted angrily. 'But there wasn't any other way. Thanks, anyway. Now we've got to go. Is he asleep, do you know?'

'Don't think so. He'd better not be. You've got to get the box while he's awake.'

Jack yelped in horror, covering his mouth to stem the noise. '*That's impossible!*'

'It's the only way. Once Saladin goes to bed, I bet it disappears with him, just in case he fancies a snack in the night. You'd never get it once the mosquito curtains are drawn, far too risky.'

Jack looked closely at the box. It certainly looked the same. In fact, if he'd been asked he'd swear it was identical to the one they were about to steal. But it wasn't – there was a difference. He peered closely. Okay, so his hand didn't gravitate towards it, and the stones in the real box had sparkled brightly in the sunlight. This just didn't have it, but perhaps it would pass in lamplight. He hoped so; their safety depended on it.

* * *

Like a moth floating on a breeze, the camel retraced his steps through the courtyard of fountains, birds singing even at night, completely oblivious of the evil surrounding them. Behind them were the kitchens, which had become their refuge and their headquarters; beneath them the dungeons, where Saleem and Prince Salah were kept, and in front of them, their destination – the ruler's quarters.

The building was massively fortified, reflecting Saladin's paranoia over the possibility of a counter-coup. Even its doors were studded with heavy bronze studs, making them almost impenetrable. But neither the guards nor the bronze studs stopped Bud. The guards slept, leaning on their spears, and the metal was of no more problem than jelly.

They emerged into a narrow entrance hall lined with trees and fountains. At any other time Jack would have looked about him, but not now. He gripped the saddle absolutely terrified. His legs were shaking so badly, he knew he couldn't have walked anywhere and wished, urgently, he was in his room with the loo near at hand. In front of him lay the gates to hell – two doors, the only things standing between him and Saladin.

He can't see us, he can't see us, he chanted to himself as the walls melted round the shape of the camel.

The room was so vast Jack's entire house could have fitted into it – its walls, floor, even part of its ceiling, pure white marble. On all four sides of the room marble pillars supported a balcony, its windows overlooking the courtyard like those in the women's quarters. Jack remembered Saleem telling him that in summer it was like a furnace and anyone, with any sense, slept upstairs by an open window, to catch any stray breeze that flowed their way.

Above the balcony soared a domed roof made from coloured panes of glass. There were windows here, too, with long chains dangling down from them, like those in old churches. The chains were threaded through an iron ratchet that was fixed to the window frame and to open or close the windows, you hauled on the chain. Several were neatly fastened back against the balcony wall, the rest left loose swinging slightly in the breeze. Dangling down from the centre of the dome was a heavy iron chain, each link as big as a man's fist, supporting a glittering, crystal chandelier.

The room was empty.

Jack sighed gratefully, knowing their task had just got that much easier. It was still scary, but searching a room with Saladin in it – even if he couldn't see them! Jack shuddered feeling barbs of gooseflesh break out on his arms.

He peered round the vast space, wondering where on earth Saladin kept his possessions. His bedroom at home had a large chest for his clothes and a big cupboard, where he kept his sports gear plus hundreds of CDs and games. There was nothing like that here. The only furniture to be seen was a half-dozen elaborately carved couches, each with its own coffee table, and a series of elegant chests, inlaid with ivory motifs, like those used by pirates to store their gold. So where on earth did Saladin keep stuff? It had to be close by; surely he wouldn't ring for a servant every time he wanted a sweet. Jack thought guiltily of the box he kept hidden under his own bed, usually full of chocolate and peanuts, in case he got peckish late at night.

Perhaps it's by his bed, he thought, looking towards the curtained tent on the far side of the room. Pointed at the top and completely surrounded and covered with fine net curtains, it was enormous – big enough for a dozen people. But then so was Saladin.

On the far side, partially hidden by the curtains, was a huge dog basket. Jack looked more closely, then wished he hadn't. The basket wasn't empty, although there wasn't a dog in it. Taking up every square inch, and overflowing onto the floor, was a snake; a python with coils as wide as Jack's body, blotched blood red.

Jack flinched backwards almost falling from Bud's back, his eyes glued to the snake as it swayed rhythmically from side to side, convinced it was Saladin. The resemblance was uncanny, except that the snake was long and fat. But it had his eyes – cold, black and unblinking. Instinctively, Jack recoiled even further into the shadows.

'Bud? There's a snake,' he whispered in the camel's ear. 'Can you see it? More to the point – can it see us?'

Bud swung round, and Jack leaned down to catch his words.

'Stay still and do not talk.'

As if he were a tendril of smoke, the camel – his rider lying flat against the saddle – floated silently along the shadowy corridor that lay beneath the balcony, its pillars shielding them from the gaze of anyone in the room. Even so the snake reared, staring straight at the balcony directly above them. Jack gazed fascinated at the vast coils that wound round and round the dog basket, the snake's small head poking up from their centre. Bud moved again, and again the snake's head followed, its eyes unblinking, its forked tongue flicking in and out of its mouth

'The snake knows there is something,' Bud kept his voice to a murmur. 'It is tracking our movement, but it cannot see us.'

'You sure about that?' whispered Jack. 'It can't be Saladin, can it? It looks just like him.'

'No infidel! This vile creature has to be one created by the dark arts, doubtless its purpose to protect Saladin from intruders. Keep silent, for it possesses powers beyond my understanding.'

'*Something else! What? Bud, let's go I beg you.*'

'Infidel, sit silently; we have to find the box.'

Jack sat, for there was nothing else he could do, his eyes constantly swivelling round to watch the snake. It was gross; its tongue flicking in and out like a giant flycatcher, its huge coils spilling out over the sides of the basket onto the floor.

He shuddered, burying his face in the saddlecloths, trying to escape its blank, hypnotic stare. It was up to Bud now, 'cos he couldn't move. If he did he'd be sick, his stomach already churning round and round. Even with his face hidden, he could still feel eyes boring into his mind, searching out what he was thinking, slithering in and out of his brain, like snakes.

Then, suddenly, there were snakes. Jack, his eyes wide and staring, gazed down at the white marble floor, where hundreds of long slithering bodies were wriggling towards the camel's legs. Spatulate-shaped heads, with black virulent eyes, their tongues filled with venom, appeared over the tops of his trainers, crawling up inside his jeans and under his jacket. He watched, unable to lift a finger to stop them, as they emerged out of the sleeves of his t-shirt. They reached his neck slithering upwards, until they were in his ears making them itch. He clamped his mouth shut, as snakes – thin as wireworms – slid into his nostrils and down the back of his throat. He retched, wishing he could be sick to rid himself of their vile squirming.

They're not real; they're not real. He wanted to scream the words out loud, to scratch out his eyes and ears to stop their itching, but he couldn't. He was frozen solid, like a statue carved in white marble.

Desperately, he tried to clear his mind of the snakes, knowing they wouldn't stop until they'd discovered everything about him. They couldn't be real. The room had been empty when they entered; they had to be a hallucination. Yet they looked and felt real. Somehow he had to stop them. But how?

Jack dug his nails into the palms of his hands, forcing himself to concentrate and blot out the flesh-creeping sensation of the snakes slithering through his clothes. What he needed was something to block them with like a barricade, a wall high enough to stop them getting over.

He shut his eyes focussing on an imaginary heap of bricks, piling one on top of the other, layer after layer, in the hope of imprisoning his brain behind it. He concentrated furiously, slapping on more and more mortar, the effort making his face run with sweat. Another layer of bricks then mortar, then more bricks, growing up higgledy-piggledy like a messy pile of sandwiches bulging with filling, until all he could see was the wall, terrified it would buckle under the pressure of the snakes.

It held and, at last, his eyes were free of them. Shivering violently, he looked down at his hands – the reptiles had vanished. Cautiously, he lifted his head from the saddle and gazed slowly about him, feeling as if he had just exited a giant mincing machine through the wrong end.

The click of a latch broke the silence. Jack froze as a door in the wall opposite opened and Saladin appeared, followed by a group of people. Jack blinked in amazement at the difference in the women, whom he'd seen earlier that evening at training. There, they had resembled shapeless black tents. Now, they wore beautiful colours and jewels.

The party, talking and laughing, made their way across the room disappearing into its shadows. Hidden beneath the balcony, Jack had not noticed the curtained archway. Lamps were lit, allowing him to peep through into a second room, smaller than the first, its roof covered with climbing plants. He stared round the elegant space, his gaze drawn relentlessly towards a low table that stood by its curtained entrance, seeing the jewel-encrusted box.

'Bud,' he whispered, gasping with relief. 'It's there! I've found the box! But if I try to get to it the snake'll see me.'

'No, infidel. Do not forget you are invisible while you remain on my back. It will be but the work of a moment to change the sweetmeats. It will be good.'

'But what about Saladin? Won't he be just a tad suspicious when his box levitates and hovers in mid-air?'

'I think the Prince will not see anything. He is well occupied.'

From the garden room came sounds of music and laughter, quite out of place in a room in which there was so much evil. Leaving the safety of the shadowy arches, Bud began to cross the open space towards the box, Jack's fingers already stretching out towards it. He grabbed his elbow to stop his arm moving. The serpent's head swayed following the movement, its eyes fixed unblinking directed straight at Jack.

Pulling the duplicate box out of his saddlebag, Jack leaned down towards the table but couldn't reach it, his fingers grasping at empty air. He hesitated, gazing wildly about him, hoping for a miracle, anything that would stop him needing to dismount. But there was nothing. Reluctantly, he slid down to the floor. The jewelled box was full, the little sweetmeats oozing with honey. He opened the dummy box, hastily upturning the real one into it. Nothing happened. Impatiently, he shook the box but the cakes remained firmly stuck together.

He was vaguely aware of music in the background, but nothing else broke into his thoughts as he concentrated on the box. And, if it hadn't been so absolutely frightful, like his worst nightmare, Jack might have laughed. Perhaps one day he could laugh – but not now. Not now, not when standing on the floor shaking a box, like a pair of maracas, visible to anyone that cared to look. Angrily, he shook the box again. The sweetmeats dropped out, so suddenly and so fast his arm jerked in surprise and two of the little cakes toppled over the edge, landing plop on the floor.

Jack froze. Risking everything, he peeped through the curtained archway to where Saladin and his friends were partying. They hadn't heard but the snake had. He felt its waves of evil closing in on him again, green smoke oozing through the mortar holding the bricks together. Snake like, the smoke wove its way between Bud's legs and round his body, seeking Jack.

Burying his face in Bud's side, Jack quickly reinforced his wall with yet more mortar, trying to seal up the cracks and stop the snake controlling his mind. But it was too strong, the bricks tumbling to the ground as if a bulldozer had struck them. Jack knew then he had only seconds. He couldn't hold it back any longer. *He had to get out!*

Bending down, he grabbed the sweetmeats off the floor, stuffing them anyhow into the dummy box. Blindly, he swung himself back into the saddle, the camel already moving as if he, too, couldn't withstand the evil power in that room. Silently, but fast, they crossed the marble floor heading for the main wall and the clean air of the courtyard. Holding the reins in one hand, Jack thrust the now empty container into the darkness of Bud's saddlebag, where he knew it would be safe.

Chapter Fourteen

Saladin Gets Upset

The camel came to a halt under one of the palm trees in the fountain courtyard, so Jack could wash his face and hands with cold water because, as he said, he could still feel snakes crawling over his skin.

'I feel sick, Bud!'

'Yes, little master! You did well. There was much evil in that room, even I could not stop it.'

'*Tell me about it.* I don't ever want to go there again.'

'There will be no need, for you have the box.'

Jack sat quietly under one of the trees, the night air clear and cold, trailing his hand in the fountain. Desperately tired, his eyes began to close. After a few minutes he sat up.

'Bud, I know you're going to hate me,' he said.

'Hate, infidel! What is this hate? *Most unlikely!*'

'Can we see Saleem before we go to Mersham?'

'*I have just changed my mind, infidel.* You are right. It is *most likely* I will hate you, if you persist in speaking such foolishness. I suggest, therefore, that you fight this inclination to see the Prince Saleem just as you fought the evil. There is no time.' Bud glared at the boy. 'First, we had to see Mercedes,' he muttered, '*now* Saleem. *I do not understand why you do not hold a party and invite the entire team to it.*'

'OK! OK! Don't keep on. You sound just like my mother. But I was right about Mercedes and I'm right about this, too. I know I am. He still thinks you're missing. Oh, come on, Bud, he must be feeling awful on his own. Five minutes isn't going to make any difference.

Five minutes to see Saleem and tell him what's happened, then we'll go.'

Surprisingly, Bud nodded, allowing Jack to climb up into the saddle. Without further comment, he headed for the barred doorway which heralded the short cut to Saleem's cell.

Saleem was lying face down on his bed, his arm across his face, a picture of despair.

'Saleem, it's okay, it's okay,' Jack shouted, as soon as he was visible. The boy sat up. There were dark circles round his eyes and he looked thinner than ever. Then a grin flashed across his face and he rushed across the room to hug them both.

Hell's Bloody Bells, Jack! *Am* I glad to see you. And Bud. *You're safe!* I really thought somefing had happened to you and I'd never get free.'

Laughing shakily, Jack hugged him back.

'We haven't got long and there isn't any food. I'm ever so sorry but I promise we'll visit the kitchen, the moment we get back.'

'Back! You're going to Jacob's? You've found the box. *Fantastic!* Tell me! Tell me!'

'Shut up and listen then! We've only got five minutes, and don't interrupt.'

Saleem, still clutching Jack's hand, dragged him across the box-like cell pushing him down onto the chair. As Jack described the attack by the bird, his eyes opened wider and wider with astonishment, shuddering dramatically as the full horror of venturing into Saladin's room unfolded.

'Jack, you're somefing else,' he said seriously, when the story came to an end.

Jack grinned. 'And now we've got the box, you'll soon be free and we'll be laughing about all this.'

'Inshallah!' said the camel.

All at once Jack shivered, remembering the nightmare feel of the snakes in his clothes. 'Saleem,' he begged. 'Come with us, *please*. I have an awful feeling ...' Saleem shook his head. 'No, Jack. I told you, I'm not leaving without my ...'

A huge noise erupted filling the air as if there had been an explosion.

'What's that?' Jack called to Bud in alarm.

'Our gentle Prince has discovered his jewelled box is missing.'

'Jeez, Bud, no!' he exclaimed, guiltily remembering the honey cakes on the floor. 'But Jacob?'

'That no longer matters, infidel. What does matter is reaching your room before the guards get there. Come!'

Jack leapt for the saddle. 'Guards?'

'They are already searching. That is the noise you hear. And they will search everywhere, even the women's quarters and the prisoners. My Lord Saleem, remember you know nothing. We will return as soon as it is safe to do so.'

The camel, with Jack clutching tightly to the reins, headed for the furthest wall. Getting into his stride, he literally flew along the corridor towards the courtyard.

'What do we do now, Bud?'

The corridor in front of them loomed dark and quiet against the background of noise.

'You will get into your bed and read your book – and lie, something of which you have doubtless had much practise. May the Gods preserve us?'

'You'd better thank them we hadn't already left the palace,' Jack retorted.

'I have already given my thanks for that blessing, infidel.'

Jack dragged off his shirt and jeans, pulling on his day robe which he slept in. Pushing everything under the bed, he grabbed his book and climbed in under the cover. The noise was louder. Outside he could see lights moving from room to room. He lay down pretending to read – his lamp lit, his book open.

'Bud, disappear but don't go.'

'No, infidel. Have faith.'

For the second time that night, footsteps sounded along the corridor and there was a thunderous knocking on his door. It banged open, crashing back against the wall. Jack sat up in bed, genuinely frightened. These guards, their spears at the ready, weren't here to rescue him. They rushed in shouting.

He didn't understand what they were saying but there was no ignoring the spears, pushing him against the wall. Abruptly his bed was overturned, the drawers in the chest pulled out and his clothes flung on the floor; his rucksack, its contents tipped out.

'*What's the matter?*' he shouted. 'What have I done?'

Two more guards, lining the doorway, stiffened to attention as Saladin entered.

'Prince Saladin, *what is this?* What's happened?'

Knowing that his mum always believed in his innocence when he needed her too, Jack immediately tried well-worn tactics – divert the enemy. 'Is it the shirts? If so, I left them at the football ground. Was that not right?'

Saladin paused. 'Shirts?' he whispered. 'Shirts!' No, that is correct. I said they should be left.'

'Then what is it, sir?'

Saladin looked round the room, studying each crack in the wall as if it could tell him something. He spoke to the guards.

'La!' they replied.

'It would seem we were mistaken to trouble you.' The ruler turned to leave.

'I'm sorry, sir, but I don't know what I'm supposed to have done?'

'*Supposed*, Mr Burnside,' hissed the ruler. '*I do **not** suppose.*'

Jack hid a sudden shiver. He'd be damned if he was going to show Saladin he was scared.

'*I have lost a box.*'

'A box! What type of box? There's no box here,' Jack said.

'*So I see.* Nevertheless, I have lost one.' Saladin shouted at the guards and, turning, left the room. The guards followed – leaving the door wide open.

Jack stood stock-still till the footsteps had disappeared, then walked to the door closing it quietly. As he turned round his legs buckled and he slid to the ground, trembling violently. After a minute or two, feeling stronger, he pulled himself back up on to his feet. Still trembling, he slowly began to put his things back in the drawers and re-pack his rucksack.

'Bud,' he whispered.

Instantly, a dark shadow appeared, growing and growing in size until it was large enough for the camel to stick his head out of the wall.

'Close, my Lord Burnside.'

'*Please, get us to Jacob,*' Jack begged. 'Then he can do the rescuing. I've had enough danger to last me a lifetime.'

'Yes, infidel. But for now, you must sleep. I will wake you when the palace is quiet, then we will go.'

'I can't sleep, Bud, honest; I'm much too worried.'

'Then put your head down, infidel, and feign sleep.'

Doing as he was told, Jack dragged his bed upright and climbed in. Immediately, he found himself dropping off, the events of the night exhausting him.

'Well, just ten minutes then,' he muttered and fell asleep.

The moon climbed high in the sky as if it too were interested in the goings-on in the palace. It watched brightly while the search moved from room to room, the occupants of the palace remaining wide awake, as the relentless search constantly disturbed their slumbers. Gradually, with the approach of dawn, the noise began to subside into the background, the soldiers, still searching, having reached the far distant corners of the palace.

Jack slept on, deeply and dreamlessly, exhausted by the emotions of the day, until the sun's rays, catching his face, woke him up.

Chapter Fifteen

The Sandstorm

The boys gathered round Jack, eagerly fingering the pile of shirts and shorts, and chattering excitedly to one another as he gave them out.

Inside, he felt angry and frustrated that there was nothing he could do, except play a stupid game of football. The only thing that really mattered was getting to Jacob and that hadn't happened. Bud had failed him. Still, at least his wooden statue was safe, tucked under a loose tile in the bathroom floor. Now, if there was another incident involving giant crows, he needn't panic.

'Put them on,' he mimed, wondering where Saleem was.

The goalkeeper's shirt went to Hassan, much to Iqbal's annoyance, and the Number 7 shirt to Yazim.

'You can take my place,' he said, not expecting the boy to understand him.

'Shruckran! Shruckran!' Yazim bowed low and, with a big grin, ran off, hugging the shirt to his chest.

'Yella,' shouted Jack, grabbing his whistle, another word he'd learned – let's go.

Their bare feet making no sound, the little group of boys trooped up the steps and out on to the pitch, to see Saladin's procession already approaching the stand. Instantly, they fell to the ground burying their faces.

'No,' shouted Jack and blew his whistle. 'Line up.'

He indicated what he wanted and the boys, looking terrified, obeyed. Hesitantly, they tried to make some sort of line, huddling together for support. Saladin stopped his escort and the palanquin was laboriously lowed to the ground. He stepped off, leaning on his armrest. As he did so, Hamid moved. Jack's arm shot out and, grasping the boy's wrist, pulled him back upright. Slowly Saladin moved along the line of ten players, checking their shirts and speaking to them in Arabic. The boys didn't reply. Silently, they stared straight ahead.

Saladin stopped in front of Jack. 'Mr Burnside, you are a mind reader.'

'Sir, you wanted a dress rehearsal and I thought ...'

'Yes, Mr Burnside, I know what you thought and it was correct, but you are much smarter than I gave you credit for.'

Jack bowed. There was nothing to say.

Saladin swung away and then turned back again. 'By the way the boy, Ali.'

'Yes, sir, what about him?' asked Jack nervously.

'He won't be joining you.'

Jack felt a flash of fear. 'But ...'

'*But*, Mr Burnside?' the ruler whispered. 'Surely you have no further need of him? After all, a dress rehearsal, as you put it, has to be just that, doesn't it? You will not require the boy's services for the game, so ...' Saladin hesitated then continued, his voice soft and sugary sweet. 'You are so enterprising, I have no doubt you will put on a rewarding performance.'

It was at that moment Jack decided he was going to be an actor, not a footballer. Not now, not since he'd become so adept at saying what he didn't mean, while keeping his face bland and innocent.

'Of course, sir. It'll be a great match, you'll see. I'm really looking forward to it, aren't you?' he said cheerfully.

The little group of spectators cheered as the ten boys ran on to the pitch, smart in their white shirts and black shorts, the numbers big and bold on their backs. Although, it still wasn't like the real thing.

With only ten men they were restricted to five-a-side, so Jack started the session off, as he had done every day, with drills and exercises.

He watched his little team enthusiastically stretch, running backwards, forwards and sideways, his mind churning. Did Saladin suspect something? But why Saleem? He didn't steal the box. He glanced over at the stand, where the ruler was chatting to his courtiers, no different from any other day. *Surely he wouldn't harm his own nephew, would he?*

He blew a long blast on his whistle, the boys eagerly taking their positions. They kicked off and the Tornadoes, having something to prove, immediately gained possession of the ball. They passed between them, giving the crowd a lesson in short passing and the Hurricanes no chance to win it back. He watched full of admiration as they tried to make space, moving the ball up towards the goal.

Their strategy worked well, until Yazim decided to take a hand and tackle Omar out on the left wing. One minute, Omar was standing still, his foot poised to kick the ball; the next, he was charging after Yazim already ten yards ahead. Yazim having got the ball was determined to keep it, flying along the length of the pitch towards the goal. Helplessly, Farouk and Omar tore off after him. Now only Yusef and Iqbal, the two defenders, blocked his progress towards Hassan, who could be seen moving purposely from foot to foot in the goalmouth. They zoomed in, both larger than Yazim and much more menacing. Yazim watched them carefully, not hesitating at all in his run. He feinted, changed direction and, breaking away, was free to shoot – GOAL!

The Hurricanes, including Yazim, rushed into a huddle, slapping one another on the back. Jack blew his whistle forcefully, trying to restore order and, after a few minutes, the four boys – Majuud, Hamid, Yazim and Sadiq – walked back to their places; Yazim, his chest puffed out like a pigeon's. Sentries on the ramparts laughed and joked. Jack saw bets being exchanged, coins passing from hand to hand, turning their practise session into a festival.

It was amazing how much difference wearing shorts made, the boys running so much faster. At long last Yazim, in particular, could watch the opposition without worrying where the ball was. A feeling of confidence swept over Jack. He gazed proudly at the boy, knowing that if he played this well in the match, the opposition stood no chance. If only the whole adventure had been about football, what fun it would have been; not scary or menacing.

They started again, the boys eagerly running to their places on the pitch, the Tornadoes determined on revenge.

Suddenly, without warning, the brightness of the sun began to disappear. One minute, a bright golden globe in a cloudless blue sky; the next, a dark, murky ball of deep brown, snuffed out by a great wind, which sucked up the loose sand from the hills above. It closed in, heading straight for the football pitch and devouring everything that lay in its path – sand – earth – leaves – stones. From all sides, great waves of spiky, sharp, tearing black dust rolled towards them.

Jack stood and watched the sky change colour. On the palace ramparts, the sentries had spotted the storm heading their way and shouted a warning. He heard the commotion and turned round, startled to see spectators rushing about in confusion. They shouted to him but he didn't understand. Suddenly – as if he'd been struck by lightning – he realised what they were shouting.

'Sandstorm!' he yelled and began to run, calling on his team to get into the stand. The air was swirling about them. Gusts tore at their faces and particles of sand, like a million knives, cut their bare legs and arms. No one could run now! Pushed back by the force of the wind, their only escape was to hide in the ground and cover their faces. Jack fell down huddling into the sand, the wind howling and screaming around him.

Gradually, the air became as black as night and a further sound added itself to the noise of the wind – a steady swishing as if someone was beating a carpet. Too late, Jack recognised the sound of wings.

He caught a scream of pain and jumped up, spreading his fingers across his face to shield his eyes. Squinting painfully through the dust, he made out the vague shape of a huge bird attacking one of his team. The boy screamed again. Jack could see him struggling desperately, trying to free himself from the monstrous talons gripping his back. He watched helplessly, pushed back by the swirling wind as the great power of the bird lifted the boy clear of the ground.

'*No! Not again!*' he yelled. Oblivious of the sand flying into his face, he forced himself forward. Too late! The powerful wings had done their job, carrying the struggling boy over the walls and into the darkness of the storm.

Jack stood there, not caring about the sand flying into his face, his eyes shut and his fists clenched. He wanted to scream out loud but couldn't, his mouth full of sand and grit. Then, as if he had pushed a switch, the wind ceased its howling and stopped blowing, and the sand stopped flying. It fell to the ground and lay still as the dark storm clouds passed away from the sun. He opened his eyes and looked about him. Once again, the sun shone steadily in a blue sky and all was silent.

The boys picked themselves up off the ground and clustered round, shouting and plucking at his clothes. For a moment, Jack couldn't get his mind back in gear; he had to though, it was up to him. He looked up at the enclosure. Nothing could be seen of Saladin, a wall of men with swords blocking his view. Jack felt for his whistle and spat, blowing a faltering blast to get silence while he checked the numbers on their shirts: 1 –2 – 3 – 4 – 5 – 6 … 8 – 9 – 10! He checked again, looking about him hopefully, wondering if the boy had made it into the stand. Then, a feeling of absolute terror swept over him as he understood the significance of what the boys had been shouting …

Number 7! Number 7! Number 7!

It had been number 7, little Yazim, whom the crow had taken.

There would be no game that morning. The boys were all too shaken and several were openly crying. Jack pushed them off the pitch and into the stand, herding them down the steps to the locker room, to get water and wash the sand from their faces. Hurriedly, they took off their prized shirts and shorts, folding them carefully and, taking their tunics from their pegs, dressed themselves again in their anonymous white robes. White robes that had no numbers on the back, so the bird couldn't identify them if it returned. Omar picked up Jack's tunic and held it out, his gesture confirming what Jack had already guessed … the bird had captured Yazim in mistake for him.

There was silence. No one spoke. The boys looked at him sadly, their faces streaked with sand and tears. What Jack would have given to have Saleem with them, able to speak to the team and comfort them. He got up, slowly moving among the nine boys – all that was left of his team – patting them on the back. Then, leaving them, he walked back up the steps and made his way to the enclosure.

* * *

The wall of guards parted reluctantly. Behind them, Saladin, his face covered with a silk handkerchief, rocked to-and-fro, keening.

'Prince Saladin?' A white and pasty face peeped at him from behind the handkerchief. 'Prince Saladin, we have lost a player. The bird took him.'

'Aaaah!' The high-pitched wailing noise began again and Jack realised the Prince was terrified.

'Prince Saladin! Whatever you think, this has got to be Sheikh

Mendorun's work. It makes no sense otherwise. And, right now, he's probably congratulating himself that he's finally wrecked the game, because he thinks he's got me.'

Saladin peeped at him from a corner of the handkerchief. 'You! *Why you?*'

'It was the boy wearing the number 7 shirt, sir, my shirt!'

'Aaaah!'

'I'm positive he won't try anything else. By the time he realises his mistake, it will be too late to plan anything. And we can still play, sir. We may not win but we can try. And, surely, he'll return the boy after the game.'

The Prince squinted round his handkerchief, his face sweating profusely. He mopped his face. 'Yes, we can still play with ten men. And I was so hopeful ... Ah, I might have known.' His voice sounded a little stronger, as if he were coming to terms with the situation.

'We can still have eleven men, if you use Ali.'

'Who?' Saladin's expression was blank, his eyes not focussing.

'The boy who speaks English. I've seen him handle the ball. He's good and Mendorun doesn't know about him.'

'Ali?'

One of his courtiers whispered in his ear. Saladin swung round, shouting angrily at the man. He turned back to Jack.

'Yes, yes, I forgot. Even that may be a possibility under such extreme circumstances. Now, I must leave you. Continue your rehearsal. If, as you say, there is no further danger, then you may continue.'

Jack watched as Saladin hurriedly left the ground ringed by his guards.

'*You rotten sleaze-bag,*' he called after him, blazing angry, no longer caring if he was understood or not. 'You're not the only one who's upset. We all are. And I thought rulers were supposed to be fearless.'

131

After Saladin's hasty departure, his courtiers had not stayed either. One by one they disappeared, seeking the safety of the palace walls. Jack tried to get his team moving but the boys ignored him, their eyes fixed on the skies – searching – not caring where the ball was. It was crystal clear that all they wanted was to get into a room where there was no sky.

Chapter Sixteen

The All-Powerful Box

It was absolutely thrilling to be out of the palace, the landscape vast and desolate, only an occasional shape of a bush breaking the flat monotony of the desert. Yet here Jack felt safe, not having to watch over his shoulder every second in case he said the wrong thing. He breathed in the clean, cold night air, glad to get away from all the danger, immediately feeling guilty because he'd left Saleem behind; even Mercedes failing to persuade him.

'It's this Prince-thing,' she explained airily. 'Saleem might be dead scared but he's more scared of givin' in to it.'

'Then you'd better come with me, Mercedes.'

'You've gotta be jokin'. I can't possibly leave now. It's just gettin' excitin'.'

Jack comforted himself that, at least, he'd tried. He looked at his watch – it was well after midnight – and wasted a whole hour trying.

He huddled closer into the saddle rugs as Bud increased his pace, soaring silently over the ground, his pathway lit by shafts of light from a new moon, now overhead. Shortly afterwards, the lights of Mersham came into view. They had travelled the distance that took Jacob and his steed nearly a whole day, in a little over half an hour.

Bud slowed, striding more leisurely along the ground between the sleeping houses, the same houses Jack had first seen six nights ago. It was warmer here, amazingly so, simply a warm tropical night; none of the inhabitants dreaming of the magic and sorcery that existed in their small town.

They entered the dark stable. Instantly, a light flared, and Jack could see the merchant, his shoulders hunched up to protect his neck, his hands cast up to the heavens – as if explaining to them, he was not responsible for anything.

'At last, you decaying mass of putrid camel-flesh, pestilence and plague on you.' Jacob stood in front of them, his hands a blur of speed, demonstrating his extreme concern. 'But *you* are most welcome, my Lord Burnside,' he continued, his voice dropping smoothly down an octave. 'I am thankful to see your safe return. You have news?'

'Yes, Jacob, there's so much to tell you. We found Saleem and Mercedes and …'

'Where are they?' Jacob gazed round the dimly lit stable, a puzzled frown on his face.

'Well, they refused to leave and then …'

'Refused to leave! *Refused to leave!*' repeated Jacob, sounding bewildered.

'*Refused to leave*! Is there something strange in those words, oh accurs-ed one, that you are forced to go on repeating them, like a parrot.'

Jack, judging World War III was just about to break out, thought it time to sue for peace. 'Bud, *for Pete's sake, give it a rest*. What's the matter with you?'

'I have barely eaten in six days,' grumbled the camel. 'Can't you feel my hump getting softer as I am denied sustenance. Surely, my Lord Burnside, with a love of food as great as your own, even you would feel irritable after six days of starvation,' he added insultingly.

Jack grinned. 'Sorry, Bud. He's right, Jacob, it's no wonder he's crabby. Can you get him some food and I'll tell you what's been happening.'

Jacob picked up a bale of hay, tossing it towards the wall, the camel's head instantly disappearing to avoid being used as a coconut-shy.

'It is good that you worry about this piece of carrion,' Jacob muttered. 'And you, my Lord?'

'A drink, and if there's any food, please?'

'But, of course, my Lord. Talk while I bring the food.'

'We found Saleem and I managed to get him out of prison during the day, to act as interpreter. And then we found Prince Salah …'

'*Sal-ah!* He's *alive?*'

The camel nodded, poking his nose out of the wall to reach the hay.

'A-ah – you have done well, beast!'

'The Gods be praised! I have waited thousands of years to hear such gratitude.'

The merchant turned and looked at Jack, his eyes boring into him. 'And Mercedes?'

'She's fine, honest,' said Jack hastily, not daring to say anything further in case Bud made a comment about Mercedes' weight, causing war to break out again. 'She helped us find the box.'

'*My box!* You have my box?' Jacob's screeched, his eyebrows soaring upwards like his voice.

Jack nodded. 'But there's more, Jacob.'

'*Tell me*, leave nothing out.'

The story took some telling, Jacob constantly interrupting and asking many questions. He turned to the camel, speaking to him in a strange language. Jack thought it resembled Arabic, recognising, 'aiwa' and la', words that Saleem had told him meant 'yes' and 'no'.

He munched on one of his favourite honey sweetmeats – the juice dripping in thick crystal rivulets down his chin, waiting impatiently for a pause in the conversation.

'Please will you speak English?' he demanded finally when it showed no sign of stopping, 'then at least I can follow. After all, I'm in this up to my neck or had you forgotten?'

'A-thousand-pardons, my Lord. It is merely that our language flows more easily on the tongue. From what the beast has been saying, you have indeed faced many difficulties and with great courage. The Gods be prais-ed that you are all safe and unharmed. Ah!' Jacob's hands flew into the air. 'I see you have questions, for which you need answers.'

'You bet I do. You only told me half a story and you never said it would be this dangerous.'

'And yet you have succeeded despite knowing so little.'

Jacob crossed the room seating himself at the table opposite Jack, his eyes once again hooded and half-closed.

'That's not the point, Jacob. You should have told me everything.'

'And had I burdened you with the truth, would you have gone?'

Jack sat silently for a moment. 'Probably not,' he admitted.

Jacob shrugged raising his hands, palms outstretched, high into the air. 'So there is no harm done! Indeed much good has come from not telling you the truth.'

Jack laughed, his anger evaporating as quickly as it had begun. He was beginning to get to know this man who used so much flattery to get his own way.

'Still I'd like to hear it now. Even Prince Salah wondered why you sent me, when you could have easily gone yourself.'

'Indeed I did, my Lord. As soon as it was safe, I searched the palace. Night after night I travelled from Mersham to no avail. I found my daughter but no sign of my Lord Prince or Saleem. To continue, I needed someone in the palace who could move about freely.'

'Saleem was taken away,' Jack explained. 'He was only brought back a few weeks ago and only then because Saladin needed Saleem to acknowledge him as the rightful ruler.'

'And Saleem?' said Jacob.

Jack grinned. 'Told him to go to hell. That's why he landed up in a cell.'

'Ah! So that is why.'

Jack sat silently, allowing all the bits to fall into place.

'Why is the box so important?' he asked after a moment. 'Prince Salah says it contains a lot of power.'

'As you will see, my Lord Burnside. My own skills are as nothing by comparison.'

'And Mendorun?'

'We know little about him, my Lord. But what we know is not good.' Jacob paused and sat down on a bale of hay, Bud noisily chewing in the background. 'He appeared in Tigrit some years ago, from where we cannot say. We know he possesses great wealth and has built a fortress in the mountains, where he maintains an army. He is the virtual ruler of Tigrit and since his appearance the kingdom has never won a match.'

'Is he responsible for the birds?'

'I believe that to be so, my Lord Burnside. I can think of no other explanation. That he is skilled in the dark arts now appears beyond question, as you yourself have witnessed. *But why would he go to such lengths to win a small game of football?* That is a question I cannot answer.'

'Perhaps he hates losing. Saleem said he wouldn't let us win whatever he had to do.'

'Perhaps,' Jacob shrugged. 'I have known of only one other and he is dead. But this is most troublesome and may yet overturn my plans to rescue the Prince Sal-ah.'

'And the snake?'

'That creature is also a manifestation of the black arts. It is doubtless responsible for Saladin becoming aware that someone had broken into his quarters.'

'I hope you're right. I thought it was me, 'cos I dropped some of the cakes,' Jack confessed.

The merchant shook his head. 'You were not to blame, my Lord.'

Jacob sat silently for a moment, his eyes veiled, thinking deeply within himself. He stirred lifting his head, his hands once again whirring round and round in their familiar restless movement.

'Now, it is time for us all to return, so you may rescue the young prince and bring him to safety.'

'Tonight?'

Jacob shook his head. 'My army like that curs-ed beast need darkness. Dawn will be upon us all too soon. You have the box?' He flashed his bird-like glance at Jack.

He nodded, darting to the saddlebag. 'It's a bit sticky inside. Saladin kept his sweets in it.'

Jacob wasn't listening, his eyes fixed on the box as if it contained all the jewels in the world, instead of the residue of honey sweets. He began to stroke its lid, speaking softly in a language Jack had never heard before and, placing the box on the ground, opened it.

'Now, I will put you to work. Come!'

For a second or two, it was if everything had been suspended in time. Not a sound. Not even a breath. Smoke began to rise from the box drifting slowly into the air, circling round and round. Gathering speed, it swirled faster and faster so that a whirlpool grew outwards from its centre. Spiralling upwards and obscuring the light, monstrous shadows began ricocheting round the room.

Jacob faced the wall all the while uttering some strange sounding words. Nothing happened. Then, curiously, the shadows on the far wall began to flicker, their shape changing, growing and swelling. One minute, they were simply reflections of a chair, a table, pots or pans; the next, silhouettes of fighting men. Men dressed from top-to-toe in darkest brown, so dark it was almost black. Their faces, swathed in deep maroon head-wraps – the Keffiyeh – were partially obscured, only their eyes, like living coals, visible. They carried staves strapped to their backs and long curved swords, which were housed in a scabbard hanging from their belt.

Trembling with fright, Jack stepped backwards, putting his hand on Bud's harness for safety.

The shadows began to move stepping out of the wall; line after line – a dozen, another dozen and then another – all in rigid formation. In a perfection of timing they bowed low to their master and, entering the whirlpool of smoke, disappeared. Jack watched speechless until the final warrior had vanished from sight and Jacob, leaning down, had closed the box.

'I told you he was tricky,' said Bud mournfully, breaking the enchanted silence of the room.

'But not this tricky,' laughed Jack shakily. 'Who are those men?'

'Why they are Riffs, my Lord Burnside,' said Jacob cheerfully. 'The legendary warriors of the desert, who appear only when evil threatens. And, indeed, we shall have great need of them.'

'But what did you say?'

'It is an ancient language, unknown today. *Manjilah vi Tubisaydah, Calulatis Im bumliaba e guilatis zur beenazah,*' Jacob repeated. gazing intently at Jack all the while. 'The words translate as, *Warriors of the Gods, Step into the light and vanquish your enemies.*'

Jacob turned away clapping his hands together.

'What now? More magic?' breathed Jack.

'No, my Lord, simply a beast of burden.'

As he spoke, a camel sidled out of the shadows on the wall and spat.

'Not another Bud?' said Jack, absolutely thrilled.

'Huh!' snorted Bud contemptuously.

'Similar, my Lord Burnside, but of a less evil disposition.'

'You forget, old man, that he's not made in my mould. *And* he can't talk,' sneered Bud. 'The accurs-ed one – who has little understanding of the nature of beasts – shut him up.'

'Why?' asked Jack, intrigued.

'Who knows,' replied Bud, with a superior smirk. 'Perhaps it kicked or bit him. Who knows what the accurs-ed one will do when he's feeling depressed.'

'And I'll shut you up too – you disease-ridden, four-legged baboon – if you say one more word.'

'Then who would you talk to, old man, when you hatch your plots.'

'Oh, Jehovah, rid me of this curs-ed monstrosity, who blights my life.' As he spoke, Jacob's voice spiralled higher and higher, resembling the whirlpool of smoke, his hands washing themselves vigorously whilst Bud calmly continued to eat.

Jack, if he hadn't been so anxious to get going, would have been happy to watch the bout knowing, if bets were taken, he'd put his money on Bud.

'Hello,' he shouted. 'We've got some serious stuff to deal with.'

'Yes, my Lord,' replied Jacob, 'serious indeed, as I am about to tell you. Tomorrow as dusk descends, the palace will open its gates to families from Tigrit. While the match is being played, we will secure the road into the kingdom. Darkness and silence will be our weapon, for none can know of our presence until Prince Sal-ah is freed from his shackles and taken to safety. When the visitors return to their homes, the Riffs will overpower the palace from inside as Saladin once did.'

Jacob paused frowning. 'Nothing, *but nothing*, must stop this match going ahead. All must seem normal. If Saladin is forewarned …' He stopped, his shoulders raised, his palms outstretched.

Jack nodded slowly. 'But you've got to get him.'

'You may leave that to me, my Lord Burnside, for I, too, have a reason to find this man. For what he has done to his brother, he will not be forgiven.'

Jack shivered, all of a sudden glad that he and Jacob were on the same side. 'And that will be it? There won't be any fighting, will there?'

'Not for you, my Lord Burnside, except the fight you will have on the football field. But do not expect to win, for you are not meant to win. Come, let us go.'

* * *

For the second and final time, Jack undertook the journey to the palace. The monotony of the landscape may have been exactly the same, but here all resemblance ended. He was no longer a timid boy chasing an adventure. Now, he was part of an army planning a daring rescue. He imagined Richard the Lion Heart, on a crusade, riding at the head of his army. Was this what it felt like, a great big fire of determination burning inside you? Carried away by his imagination, he kicked his heels into Bud's ribs to make him go faster.

'Excuse me, infidel, is that how you treat your friends, to kick them in the ribs?'

'Sorry, Bud,' said Jack guiltily. 'I was daydreaming.'

'If I may say so, dreaming of any kind will be distinctly dangerous for the next few hours. May I urge total wakefulness and no rib kicking – unless it is to the enemy – and then you will have my blessing.'

'Yeah, I agree,' Jack laughed, leaning down to pat the camel.

The walls of the palace loomed in front of them. Jack looked about him anxiously but all was in darkness, his absence still undiscovered.

'Where do you go now, Jacob?' he asked.

'To make sure all is prepared. Then, and only then, will I seek the Prince Sal-ah, to tell him that deliverance is at hand.'

'And me?'

'I believe, my Lord Burnside, that you should go to bed and sleep. For you, tomorrow will be a long day and you will need all your strength. However, before I leave you, there is something I need you to do.'

Bud snorted. 'There always is,' he muttered gloomily.

'Please give this to Mercedes.' Jacob passed a package to Jack.

'Is that all?' said Jack disappointed.

Jacob nodded. 'Yes, my Lord, but do not forget it, and remember all I have told you.'

Jacob's voice descended to a new depth. Jack stared transfixed as the merchant's outline began to change, exactly as the shadows on the wall had changed only an hour since. He blinked in disbelief, rubbing his eyes. But no, it wasn't his imagination. The man was straightening up, his hands steady on the reins. Why, he even looked taller and heavier, and his eyes were no longer shifty but glinting and full of fire.

In silence, the two camels stopped before the outer walls of the palace.

'*Salaam! Peace, be with you, my Lord Burnside!* We will meet next under happier circumstances,' cried Jacob, disappearing with his mount in the direction of the mountain pass.

'I hope you're not going to do that, Bud.'

'Infidel?'

'Grow ten centimetres.'

'A mere trick of the light,' replied Bud scornfully, heading for Jack's bedroom.

'Some trick!'

Chapter Seventeen

The Football Match

The stand was full of noisy spectators, the tall floodlights illuminating the ground and the spectators – in their black and white robes – like day.

Jack looked round him and a feeling of real pride surged through his body, like warm blood running through his veins. *He'd done it!* He'd actually carried off the impersonation for seven whole days without being found out. It had been great being top dog and telling everyone else what to do. They were nice kids and he almost wished he could take them back with him to Birmingham and let them play for his team there.

His team looked better, chattering among themselves and peering excitedly at the crowd in the stand. Jack heard the click of the gate opening and automatically looked up, his face breaking into a smile. It was Saleem, accompanied by his guards but free to play none the less. The boys flocked to him en mass, surrounding him, all talking together in a babble of excited noise.

Finally, with a loud imperious crash that startled the spectators into silence, the gate was flung back against the wall and bodyguards appeared, followed by the royal procession. The Prince and his guest, each of them carried on the shoulders of four strong men, were seated among garlands of flowers, high above the dozens of courtiers and servants marching on either side.

Jack looked keenly at the archenemy, Mendorun, who had tried so hard to scupper the match. The exact opposite of Saladin, he was tall and very thin, with greying hair, quite different from the oily blackness of Saladin's. Slashed across one side of his handsome hawk-like face ran two deep and very prominent scars. Astonished, Jack watched the two rulers chatting as if they were on the friendliest of terms, which was quite bizarre after the nightmarish happenings of the last couple of days.

The teams ran out on to the pitch, Jack allowing Hassan the honour of leading them and fitting himself into the middle of the rank where he would be less conspicuous. He inspected the officials closely. Saladin's interpreter was working one of the sidelines but the others, including the referee, belonged to the opposing camp. *Hope he's fair*, Jack thought, taking up his position.

The referee's whistle sounded and, ten minutes later, Jack realised the last thing on the referee's mind was fairness. By half-time, with the score at one-all, Jack had almost become resigned to the violence, simply hoping he'd have enough men left standing to play the second half.

'Now look,' he ordered, as the team clustered round him. 'We can win this, but we have to be even quicker than in the first half, and keep away from the other side. No contact, do you understand?'

Saleem translated, the boys nodding – Iqbal and Farouk grimacing cheerfully as they rubbed their bruises.

'Exactly,' said Jack. 'Go for the long pass, like we practised last night, remember? Keep the ball moving; it'll wear the other side out and keep them away from us. Our main problem is staying out of trouble. The way this ref works, if we breathe on the opposition he'll give them a penalty; if they foul us, he won't.'

'Ali,' he said, looking across at Saleem. 'That right defender is slow. If you get a chance, go in that way. Omar, Majuud – keep your eye on Ali. If he goes up that left wing, keep their defenders away from him.'

The only trouble with a half-time chat, the opposition had a half-

144

time chat, too. Jack watched helplessly as they worked the ball on the far side of the pitch. He snatched a glance at the front row of the stand, where the two rulers sat in isolated splendour. Mendorun sat upright, rigidly watching, not a flicker of emotion on his face; while Saladin lolled back in his seat, stuffing sweetmeats into his mouth. *So far so good,* Jack thought suddenly nervous, butterflies dodging bullets in his belly, praying that Jacob had guessed the outcome correctly.

'Course he will,' he muttered, thinking of the shadowy warriors. 'Course he will.'

Suddenly, a mistimed kick brought the ball winging his way. Jack raced after it, picking it up with his right foot, turning as he did so and heading towards the goal. *Anyone about?* He flicked a glance over his shoulder as two boys circled round him, like hyenas waiting to attack. Omar was there. Collecting the chest-high pass, Omar made a few yards down the pitch, leaving Jack to lose his shadows and get back into position to take the ball on again. But, at the last second, Omar found himself on the ground, with the ball speeding on its way towards the other half.

Damn! Jack raced back up the wing, crossing the same turf he had flown over with the ball a couple of seconds before. He checked the clock on the front of the stand.

Twenty minutes.

Now Hassan was being besieged, five players surrounding the goalkeeper, trying to intimidate him into making a mistake. Sadiq and Ahmed were doing their best to block them. Arms akimbo, they darted from side to side, while Iqbal and Yusef – his dream team – stood shoulder to shoulder with Hassan, refusing to let the ball past them. And you could tell, it would reach the net only over their dead bodies.

The tension round the ground was building to breaking point. Someone would crack unless he got the ball clear. Jack sneaked in as the ball ricocheted off the goalpost and, getting his right foot to it, sent it twenty yards to Hamid, waiting in mid-field unmarked. And Hamid, determined not to let his team-mates down, managed to clear the ball down the field and out of danger.

Next second, Jack was toppled to the ground, winded by a vicious punch. No whistle sounded to stop the game and only Ahmed ran over to help him, as play moved away down the pitch. He lay there for a minute gasping like a fish on dry land, before slowly getting to his feet. He hobbled after the ball, holding his side to ease the pain. At least he was on his feet and could watch what was happening, even if he couldn't run.

Fifteen minutes!

The ball was away down on the left wing now, Majuud taking it into the top third of the field.

'Come on, Majuud, get it to Saleem,' Jack muttered.

But Majuud – not able to hear – thought differently, trying to reach the goal himself. He lost it in a tackle and the defender kicked it back up the pitch, the ball soaring high into the air with no one about to pick it up.

'Right into my lap,' grinned Jack, catching it on his chest bone, so that it lost its pace and obediently dropped to the ground. Taking his time he jogged quietly along, letting the field sort itself out. Omar was free in the centre and he safely passed to him, while he doubled back on himself to lose his approaching escort, picking up the ball again from a neat pass back from Omar.

Ten minutes left!

Breath back. NOW GO!

Jack flew down the centre of the pitch, praying that at least Saleem would be there. He glanced round behind him, three in front between him and the goal, his faithful shadows hard on his heels.

'OK, Saleem, let's show'em,' he muttered.

He passed to Saleem, who swiftly edged the ball out to Majuud. No mistake this time. Jack, making his move and wrong footing his shadows, ran completely round them, to arrive five yards from the goalmouth. The ball – high and wide – came in from Majuud. Then, to Jack's utter disbelief, Farouk, not realising Jack was behind him, intercepted and, taking the header, nodded it straight into the hands of the keeper.

'Damn!'

Jack set off after it, outrunning the opposition as Iqbal, once again, intercepted the long pass from their keeper and sent it back to him.

'This time do it right,' he shouted impatiently and, sidestepping his shadows, passed to Farouk.

For a moment Majuud remained unmarked on the left wing and he efficiently picked up the pass from Farouk but, before he could make a move, two defenders closed in on him, one either side. Panicking, he gazed towards Saleem and Omar, only to find them both tightly cornered and unable to help. Thinking fast, Majuud sent the ball high and long back up the pitch, the spectators, their heads flying from right to left and left to right, following the run of the ball.

All attention was now focussed on Sadiq. Supporters watched with bated breath as both midfielders and forwards closed in on him. Having practised the manoeuvre, Sadiq knew he had to get the ball back to Majuud, giving Jack enough time to get into position. He waited, dribbling the ball gently from foot to foot, trying to time his kick.

Now!

He struck the ball cleanly. It flew past the players converging on him all the way to Majuud's feet, leaving him clear to strike the ball towards the goal. It was a solid cross kick which Jack, using his full height easily took possession, nodding it at the keeper. The boy got the tips of his fingers to it, but it was not enough. The ball was over the line and in!

GOAL! TWO-ONE!

Four minutes to go!

Anyone can survive four minutes, thought Jack, walking slowly back to his position. Next second he was eating his words as Omar hit the ground. Jack didn't even glance at the referee. *Wasn't worth it.*

Three minutes to go!

The ball headed once again for their goal, eight of the opposing team banding together to launch an all-out attack. Jack, flying down the pitch to help, saw that Ahmed, Iqbal, Yusef and Sadiq had already joined Hassan. The goal mouth began to resemble a herd of stampeding cattle; feet and arms working overtime – shirts pulled – sly kicks and punches – defenders ducking and diving, their eyes chasing the ball. Jack wondered how they were managing it, but so far they were keeping their heads as, time and time again, the ball headed for the goalmouth.

TIME! IT'S BLOODY TIME!

Still the whistle didn't sound.

Out of the corner of his eye, Jack saw the ball speeding towards Sadiq, directly in front of the goalmouth. He flung himself at it, his left foot getting a touch, enough to deflect the angle of the ball. He was after it again in a flash, beating two of his opponents and, picking it up again with his left foot, took on the entire attack, dodging and twisting – exactly like a rugby player heading for a touchdown – anything to get the ball clear. A sudden twist gave him space enough to take the shot.

'OK, ref, now blow your whistle!' he shouted, blasting the ball towards Saleem, clear down the pitch on the left wing, with nothing but two defenders and the keeper between him and the goal.

The whistle instantly sounded.

'Told you so,' he said, a broad grin on his face.

His team clustered round him, thumping each other on the back and grinning from ear to ear. Jack glanced up at the stand. Three-quarters of the spectators were cheering and even Saladin was on his feet, taking the congratulations of his courtiers.

A feeling of marvellous euphoria swept through Jack. He went over to his opposition, shaking hands and smiling, happily ignoring their angry looks. *I've done it! I've only gone and done it! And if I can do this,* he told himself, still wanting to turn cartwheels of joy, *I can do anything.*

The two teams lined up in front of the stand, the home crowd still cheering, unable to believe that after so long the kingdom had actually won a match. Saladin bowed graciously to the cheering crowd, as if he was personally responsible for the goal, before presenting the small silver cup to Hassan, who accepted it nervously. Then, the twenty-two players, Jack included, followed by the officials, slowly passed in front of the ruler so he could shake hands with them all.

After that, the excited players made their way across the ground, Jack at their head, and down into the locker room to change. His team chattered and laughed and Jack, even not understanding the words, knew that a blow-by-blow account was going on. He looked proudly at the ten boys, happy that Saleem had been given the freedom to play.

Without warning, the locker room door banged open and guards appeared, shouting at Saleem to get a move on. For a brief second, Saleem looked frightened. Then he caught sight of the shocked faces of the beaten team, huddled together in a corner of the locker room, and shrugged.

'I bet they think we put all our heroes in jail,' he called across the room to Jack. 'Not after tonight,' Jack shouted back, knowing only Saleem would understand and determined to let him know what was about to happen.

Saleem's face changed dramatically. 'Thanks,' he called again and gave Jack the thumbs up. 'See yer,' and putting on his tunic, disappeared through the door.

A moment later and Jack was ready, too. Collecting his gear, he left the still chattering boys in the locker room and went out, climbing back up the steps.

Spectators roamed the stands, gathered in groups, talking, chatting and laughing, as families met up again. Saladin talked and laughed too surrounded by his people. Only Mendorun sat alone, silent and still, like a statue. Abruptly he turned, staring across the empty space – straight at Jack.

Jack felt the eyes before he saw them, their hypnotic power drawing his own upwards. At that moment the game was over. Mendorun forced Jack's eyes up, forging an invisible chain with his own, boring into him like a giant crushing machine. Jack, tired now and off-guard, realised too late the danger he was in. Desperately he strove to break the contact and tear his eyes away. Already, he could feel the tendrils of evil twisting and turning as they searched out his thoughts.

Suddenly Mendorun shouted, pointing straight at Jack. '*Here is your traitor*,' he shouted in English, so Jack would understand. 'This is not your footballer.'

Jack felt his skin being torn away as if it was a latex mask, stripped away to expose someone completely different. Jacob's disguise had vanished. Now it was at him, the real Jack Burnside, that everyone was looking.

Saladin turned to stare. Mendorun shouted again this time in Arabic, loudly and forcefully, still pointing at Jack. Jack watched as sentries, their spears at the ready, converged on him. He tore his gaze away from Mendorun, looking wildly over the heads of the crowd towards the gate. He'd never reach it; it was too far away. He was surrounded.

Bloody hell fire! I'm not giving up now. Not now, not when I've just won the match for Saladin. Surely, he won't lock me up now?

Even as the thought took shape, Jack knew the answer. His face empty of all emotion, he stayed where he was, waiting for the spears to march him into the dungeons as they had Saleem.

Then, amazingly, there were nine chattering and laughing footballers between him and the sentries.

'Shruckran!' he yelled as he ran. They'd given him enough time to get to the gate and, if he got to the gate, he'd get to his room.

He ran fast, ignoring the shouts behind him, pelting through the opening in the boundary wall and across the open space towards the postern, tucked away in the heavy fortress wall. His luck held. For the first time since his arrival at the palace, the gate was open, allowing visitors to pass back and forth. He lifted the latch then he was through into the courtyard. It was deserted, everyone at the match.

The shouts behind him were louder now but Jack took no notice, they just didn't have the speed, even if he had played football for an hour. He took the short cut through the narrow alley, hoping it would slow down the heavily armed men, emerging in the inner courtyard. He ran up the stairs, two at a time, and into the corridor leading to his room, his rucksack bouncing madly on his back. He slammed the door behind him and, catapulting himself into the bathroom, feverishly pulled up the tile to get at the camel.

It was there – it was safe.

He tore back into the bedroom, diving headfirst onto his bed to reach the lamp.

'COME ON, BUD, IT'S TIME TO GO,' he yelled, placing the wooden animal against the wall so the light could reflect its shadow.

Pulling out drawers he thrust clothes recklessly into his bag, watching the shadow rear up on the back wall, all the while listening to the running footsteps along the corridor.

'Infidel, perhaps next time you will not leave things quite so late.'

Jack leapt for the saddle as the door crashed open. 'Absolutely, Bud, I promise next time, I won't.'

The shadow of the camel dominated the wall, spilling over onto the ceiling. Then, before the eyes of the startled guards, it moved and vanished, leaving behind an empty room with a discarded white tunic on the bed.

Chapter Eighteen

The Rescue

Surprisingly, there was no shouting, nor running or fighting. Families strolled leisurely from the stadium and through the outer courtyard towards the main gate. There the guards scrutinised every person closely as they passed by, otherwise everything appeared as normal.

'What do we do now, Bud? There's still an awful lot of people about and I don't want to be seen.'

'You forget we cannot be seen, infidel, but we may well be heard. You are puffing like a camel that has eaten too much new grass.'

'Well, so would you, if you had men with spears chasing you,' retorted Jack. 'Anyway, shouldn't we find Jacob and tell him what's happened?'

Bud moved silently among the trees of the garden oasis, stopping deep in their leafy shadow.

'The master said to go to Mercedes and that is what we will do, but first rest and get your breath back. We cannot move freely while the lights from the football ground burn as bright as the day.'

Jack didn't argue, glad of the peace and quiet after the chase. He looked longingly at the soft grass, wishing he could lie down and go to sleep but then he would be both visible and in danger. His only safety lay in staying where he was, a mere shadow. Time passed and Jack, looking at his watch, saw they'd been waiting almost an hour. At last their patience was rewarded as, with a loud burst of energy, floodlights were switched off.

'Now we go,' said Bud heading through the trees towards the

women's quarters. They were in darkness, most of the women not yet returned from dinner in the Rainbow Hall. Mercedes was waiting, pacing up and down anxiously.

'Jack!' she whispered. 'Thank goodness! You got away. I honestly never thought you would. You sure can run.'

'Well, it's thanks to the team I did. Are they OK?'

Mercedes nodded. 'Great match, by the way. But all hell's broke loose now; I bet your ears were burnin'.'

'Burning?'

'Of course! You were the sole topic of conversation at dinner, with Saladin givin' Mendorun the third degree.'

'I don't understand,' Jack said, sounding puzzled. 'Why the third degree?'

'*Because*, lamebrain! Saladin wanted to know whether Mendorun was just a sore loser, or whether he really read your mind.'

'He read my mind,' admitted Jack reluctantly.

'I wouldn't like to have your mind, Jack – a fine mess in there …'

'It's all right for you …' he glowered.

'When you get home, I'd visit a shrink and get it cleaned-up,' continued Mercedes airily.

'Oh curs-ed child of Satan, now is not the time for levity.'

'*OK! OK! I know.* Anyhow, he's guessed you've come to rescue Saleem, with a camel and an army of shadows – somethin' like that – and that means Pops is somewhere about.'

Jack nodded. 'You're right, he is. But how do you know all this, Mercedes?'

'Because one of your little team, Yusef, I think his name was, was servin' at dinner. He heard him say so and came to tell me.'

Jack frowned. 'Why you?'

'Great Lucifer, give me strength! 'Cos servants know everythin', der brain. Didn't it ever occur to you, that your football team knew all along, it was the prince helpin' you? Course they knew. And Saleem and me are best friends.'

Astonished, Jack slowly shook his head.

'Honestly! Some people! Anyway, Saladin asked Mendorun if he can send a couple of prisoners to him for safekeepin'. It doesn't take a genius to guess what that means, *the murderous thug!*

'And?' demanded Bud.

'*And* – Mendorun agreed. Anyway, Saladin said, once they were dead any attack was bound to fail. He wasn't worried, 'cos no one could get past his bodyguard. He didn't say it quite like that, but you get the gist.'

'The snake, Bud?'

Bud's harness jingled as he nodded his agreement.

'Can I continue, if you two have *quite finished?*'

'Sorry, Mercedes.'

'So you should be,' said the girl impatiently. 'But that's not all. I overheard some of the women sayin' that Saladin is real miffed with you, because you made a fool of him. That *really* got to him, and he's dreamin' up some very nasty things to do to you, when he catches you – so he'd better not catch you. Anyhow, Bud, you get to Pops and warn him. Tell him they're usin' the old road.'

Bud bowed his head. 'We go now, mistress.'

'*Hey*, you got somethin' for me?'

'Jacob gave us a parcel, is that what you mean?' Jack pulled the package from his saddlebag and tossed it to her. 'Stay there,' he called over his shoulder as the camel broke into a trot. 'We'll be right back.'

* * *

'Bud,' shouted Jack into the wind. 'What did Mercedes mean by the old road?'

'Before the kingdom was hidden, there was a good road to the northeast towards Tigrit. That is the road they will take.'

Bud moved rapidly, flying through the brush and sand-blown shrub, both he and his rider knowing how much was at stake. In a very few minutes the mountain pass came into view. It was still and dark and looked completely deserted, a brisk desert wind echoing softly through the gorge. Above them, a pale moon flirted shyly with a colony of fluffy clouds, fading in and out to highlight jagged peaks and cliffs, like a Son et Lumière without the sound.

All at once, Jack glimpsed movement high up on the mountainside. He squinted, trying to see more clearly through the starlit darkness. The moon soared from behind a cloud lifting the shadows and he recognised the dark shape of the ghostly warriors, dangling from long ropes. A long way below was the ledge and its guardians, the brown-robed men flashing their swords, very much on guard. Excitedly, Jack watched the black shadows walking backwards down the sheer wall of the cliff, heading for the ledges where the unsuspecting guards were patrolling. They stopped about a metre above them, their feet braced against the cliff wall, freezing into immobility – like giant spiders eager to pounce on an unsuspecting fly. The last of them slid into place and, simultaneously, as if a signal had been given, they relinquished their ropes, leaping silently onto the back of their prey. There was no noise other than a series of muffled thuds, their staves battering the sentries senseless so that they fell to the ground and lay still.

Jack looked up as the stern figure of Jacob appeared on the opposite side of the gorge. He leaned forward to tell Bud, but he was already moving.

'My Lord Burnside!' exclaimed the sorcerer.

'Saladin!' gasped Jack. 'He's sending Prince Salah and Saleem to Mendorun. Hurry or we'll be too late.'

'Beast?'

'It is true, master. They take the old road to Tigrit.'

Jacob nodded. 'It is indeed as I suspected, the kingdom is once again open. No matter, men are already waiting in the mountains.'

'So all is well, master?'

Jacob nodded, turning to Jack, his eyes strong and powerful. 'My Lord Burnside, go with Mercedes and rescue Saleem. If he is already taken, send the camel to warn me. Hurry!' he commanded. 'Never fear, I will reach the mountains before Saladin's men.'

Bud wasted no time, moving as fast as he could high above the ground, the lights of the palace coming quickly into view. The main gates were open with sentries alert and on guard, the outer courtyard awash with light. Close to the bronze gate horses stood, saddled and bridled, waiting for their riders. The camel stopped by a coppice of trees close to the gates, drawing deep into their shadow, a thick canopy of leaves blocking out the moonlight.

Through the gates, Jack could just see the great doors to the tented dining room. They opened and the tall figure of Mendorun appeared, his retainers encircling him. Unable to stop himself trembling, Jack drew back behind a palm tree, terrified the power contained in Mendorun's eyes would seek him out again. The body of men made their way leisurely through the bronze gate, towards the waiting animals. They mounted, trotting across the courtyard and, once clear of the palace walls, spurred their horses to a gallop. The pounding hooves raced past them, too fast to notice the boy hidden in the shadows.

Jack heard the bronze gate close with a thunderous clang. Then, all was quiet, the visitors having now left the walled city to return home. But still the outer gates remained open. Bud stayed silent and, even though he knew they couldn't be heard, Jack felt too scared to talk. Once again, they heard the telltale clink of bridles as a dozen mounted guards appeared, their animals slow and plodding compared to the high-spirited beasts Mendorun's party had been riding. In the midst of them, surrounded on all sides, was the stooped figure of Prince Salah. Obviously weak and ill, a guard grasped at the saddle of the horse the prince was riding, to stop him falling off. Jack gasped, his hand flying to his mouth to stem the noise. Slowly the soldiers moved away, following the tracks left by the riders already several miles ahead of them.

'Where's Saleem?' Jack whispered. 'If anything's happened to him, I'll never forgive myself.'

'Then we must hurry, infidel.' The camel already moving, headed once again for the women's quarters, where Mercedes was waiting.

Except Mercedes with her long colourful gown and shawl was no longer there. In her place stood a warrior, dressed identically to the Riffs, even to the sword, only her eyes visible above the dark maroon of the keffiyeh.

'You're kidding, right!' Jack gasped, stunned by the sight.

'Can you fight?' Mercedes said calmly, as if she was proposing a walk in the country.

'If I have to.'

'You'll have to. Here!' Mercedes tossed him a stave. 'Use it. Come on, help me up. Let's go get Saleem.'

Bud, carrying the two youngsters, made his way along the courtyard to the small door, trotting down the narrow corridor to Saleem's cell. The cell door was open, it's dim light spilling into the corridor.

'We're too late, Bud, what are we going to do?' Jack groaned.

The invisible shadow entered the cell. Three guards were already there, poking their spears at something in the roof. It was Saleem. He had climbed up on the bars to escape and was successfully dodging all attempts to dislodge him. Jack sighed happily and began to enjoy the comedy, Saleem clearly a match for anyone trying to remove him from his cell.

The guards appeared to be quarrelling about something, their angry shouts reinforced by waving fists. After a few minutes the smallest of the three, still arguing, hauled himself up onto the shoulders of the other two. Immediately, he began wobbling violently, almost falling, grabbing hastily at the bar. Then, noticing he was still wearing his sword, he yanked it from its scabbard and let it fall to the ground. There was a screech of anguish from one of the guards below. Jack grimaced in sympathy, as the unlucky guard punched the air with a closed fist, vigorously rubbing at his head where the sword had hit him.

Saleem chortled and, ignoring the man now edging along the narrow iron girder towards him, stayed where he was, making no attempt to escape. Jack held his breath, knowing exactly what Saleem was planning to do. He'd done it often enough at football training, when rain had taken them inside to the gym.

The guard made a lunge for the boy's leg. Before he could grab it, Saleem dropped low on to the bar. Catching it with both hands, he swung lightly across to the parallel bar two metres away, leaving the guard spread-eagled and grasping at empty air. The man slipped and almost fell. He clung on grimly, yelling loudly to his comrades to help him down.

'Easy,' laughed Mercedes. 'You take the one on the right.'

'No,' whispered Jack. 'They can't see us, so let's disarm them. Come on, Bud.'

As Bud moved silently between the two men, Mercedes leant out to her left, Jack to his right. Before the guards knew what was happening, they had eased the swords free from their scabbards. Saleem watched as the swords rose into the air under their own steam, before disappearing. He banged his fists triumphantly into the air, aware the cavalry had at last arrived.

'OK, I'm out'a here,' he called in English. Swinging hand over hand across the cell, he dropped to the floor, back-flipping his way to the door. 'Sorry guys,' he shouted. Then, with a clang, the door was shut and the key turned in the lock.

'Come on, Bud,' Jack ordered.

Bud needed no telling. Outside, in the corridor, Saleem stood waiting. The captured swords of the enemy clattered to the ground, as the warrior and the football hero jumped off the camel's back and hugged the gymnast.

'Wow, that was great. We must do it again some time,' laughed Saleem. 'But what about my farver, is he safe?'

Jack shook his head. 'You were lucky, Saleem. He's been taken away. It's okay though,' he added quickly, watching Saleem's grin vanish and fear take over. 'Jacob's gone after him.' He patted him on the shoulder. 'He'll get him, don't worry.'

Saleem nodded soberly. 'I know he will.' He looked down at the bunch of keys in his hand. 'Jack, you see what these are?'

'Keys,' replied Jack. Then the significance of what he'd just said hit him. 'We can free the prisoners!'

'Hey, hold up you, guys,' cried Mercedes. 'Pops didn't tell you to do that, did he, Bud?'

'It wasn't in that accurs-ed megalomaniac's plan of campaign certainly – but since he isn't here to ask ...'

'Hey! Enough of the insults, you sanctimonious old beast! That's your master and don't you forget it. You can bet your life, if he didn't tell you to release the prisoners, he had his reasons.'

'Good for you, Bud,' laughed Saleem, back to his normal self. 'Glad someone's on my side. Come on, Merk. I know why he didn't want them released, because they're too weak to be any use. They'll just be in the way, if there's a fight. But do you really want them locked up a second more than necessary?'

The girl shook her head.

'That's brill! Bring the swords, Jack.'

'We need light, Saleem,' Jack suggested sensibly, 'the cells are pitch-black. The prisoners will believe it's a trick if they can't see you.'

Saleem frowned. 'OK! OK! I've got it. Bud – you and Jack – go get my lamp from the cell. It won't hurt those bullies to suffer in the dark a few hours.'

Jack, remounting Bud, vanished through the wall. He reappeared, a few seconds later, clutching the lamp and grinning madly.

'They didn't take it very well,' he chuckled. 'I expect they thought it was witchcraft when the lamp began to move through the air. I left them clutching one another and wailing.'

Mercedes giggled. 'I'd loved to have seen that. Wish I'd come with you now.'

With Bud close behind, the three young people started down the corridor; Saleem with the keys, Jack the lamp and Mercedes the swords. They reached the first of the underground dungeons and Saleem, fiddling awkwardly with the heavy bunch, tried one of the keys. It didn't turn. He chose another and then another.

'Got it,' he whispered triumphantly as the door opened. Carrying the lamp he went in, calling out to the men inside. Door after door was opened as they moved through the prison. Gradually, the space behind them filled with a ramshackle army of men; unshaven hungry men, some too weak to walk and needing help, others unable to bear even the dim light of a lamp, but all determined to get out. Saleem turned the key of the small barred gate which led into the outer courtyard. Then they were free and in the open air.

The courtyard was quiet and empty. Jack glanced up at the ramparts. Sentries patrolling. Not good. Hastily, he waved the prisoners back into the shelter of the little doorway. Too late! There came a shout of alarm as guards patrolling the battlements spotted them. A door opened further down the courtyard and guards, their swords at the ready, ran out.

Chapter Nineteen

The Desert Warriors

'Now I know why Jacob didn't want the prisoners let out,' Jack called over his shoulder. 'We've alerted the guards. *Now what do we do?*'

'Any chance of Pops turnin' up?' Mercedes said calmly, and stepped past Jack out into the courtyard.

Jack grabbed her sleeve, pulling her back into the safety of the corridor.

'Don't be stupid, Mercedes, you can't fight them on your own. *Oh, where is Jacob?*' he groaned, 'just when we need him, too.' He patted Saleem on the arm. 'It's okay though, Bud will take us to safety. Only thing is, we have to leave the prisoners.'

Saleem glared. 'No way, Jack. I'm not leaving them. What sort of prince would I be if I ran away, leaving my men to be taken prisoner again. We must fight. We have no choice.'

'Jeez, Saleem, that's all very well, but what with? There's a whole army out there.' Jack gazed bitterly at the men crowding the corridor behind him. 'This lot can hardly stand up.'

He opened the door a crack and peered out at the empty courtyard. At its far end, half a dozen sentries were moving purposely towards them, checking each door on their way.

'Jacob told me that the Riffs always appeared in times of danger,' Jack shook his head miserably. 'He was wrong about that too.'

'But young master, you have the spell. Use it.'

'The spell, Bud? What spell? I don't know any spells.' Jack stared blankly at the camel. His expression suddenly cleared. 'Oh, you mean *that spell.'* The one Jacob used, the one in that weird language. I can't remember that, can you?'

Bud shook his head gloomily. 'How can one remember everything the accurs-ed one says and does.'

'Try listenin',' growled Mercedes.

'You know it, Mercedes?'

The girl shook her head. 'Pops expected to be here, remember?'

Jack stared down at the ground frowning. 'Hang on a mo! I've got it.' He looked up excitedly. *'Warriors of the Gods, Step into the light and vanquish your enemies.* That's it, that's what he said,' he shouted.

'But that's English! That's not a weird language,' said Mercedes.

'I know that. Hang on a minute!'

In the distance marching footsteps could now be heard.

'We haven't got a minute, Jack,' said Saleem.

'OK! OK! I'm doin' my best.' Jack frowned ferociously at the wall trying to remember, all the time conscious of the approaching footsteps. All at once, the words flashed across his vision. *'Manjilah vi Tubisay ... dah!'* he mumbled. A smile of triumph flashed across his face and he repeated the words more confidently. *'Manjilah vi Tubisaydah: Warriors of the Gods! That's it! That's it!'*

Flinging open the door into the courtyard, he called loudly. *'Manjilah vi Tubisaydah C ... Calu – latis Im bumliaba e guil – atis ... zur beenazah.'*

Nothing happened, except the guards, glancing up, broke into a run, their heavy army clanking like old tins cans.

'O'er!' groaned Mercedes. 'Try it again.'

With one eye on the approaching soldiers, Jack shouted the words once more into the peaceful air of the courtyard.

'Manjilah vi Tubisaydah, Calulatis Im bumliaba e guilatis zur beenazah.'

As he spoke the moon soared majestically out of a cloud, its bright light lifting the shadows in the courtyard; shadows which began to move, twisting and turning into the shape of the desert warriors. Silently, each one removed itself from the flat stone surface of the wall, dropping to a crouch on the ground.

'Yes!' yelled Jack, punching his fist at the air. 'It's worked!' Grasping his stave firmly, he stepped confidently into the courtyard, Mercedes by his side. 'Did I underestimate Jacob!'

'Never, **never** underestimate my pops,' laughed Mercedes. 'OK, let's kick ass. Hi-yah!'

Her call echoed round the courtyard, mingling with a series of low whistles as several dozen voices answered her, and alerting the sentries patrolling the walls above them. They stared down unbelieving at the Riffs milling about the courtyard, stunned by the appearance of an enemy within the walls.

A number of the shadowy figures converged on guards approaching down the courtyard, while others could be seen running fast towards the ramparts. Safely in the lea of the wall, two of the warriors formed a platform by locking their arms around each other's shoulders. The rest dropped into a low crouching line, seemingly oblivious to the arrows hurtling down on them. As if the movement had been practised time and time again, the first in the line sped forward, tumbling into the air to land on a man-made platform. The rest followed, leaping into a high somersault to land on the shoulders of the man below. Before the eyes of the startled youngsters a living ladder sprang up, a high tower of men balancing on each other's shoulders. The last one soared into the air landing safely. Catapulting himself up on to the battlements, he dropped a length of rope to the ground. There was a ripple of black as the warriors swarmed swiftly up. Next second, the panic-stricken sentries were confronted by a silent enemy sprinting into position, their arrows now useless at such close quarters.

In the courtyard below guards, running out from the safety of their barracks to battle with the intruders, had no time to look up to see what was happening. Even so they hesitated, taken aback by the sight of such unnatural happenings; warriors with eyes that spouted fire who had seemingly appeared out of a wall. Next second, they charged, secure in the knowledge that sheer force of numbers would overwhelm the interlopers.

Mercedes unsheathed her sword in time to deflect the spear aimed at her. Jack, not a thought in his head except survival, grasped his stave firmly in both hands, gluing his eyes to the spear aimed at his chest bone. He dodged to one side, wondering how long he could keep it up. What had Andy once said about watching your opponent's eyes? Timidly, he raised his eyes staring at his attacker and caught the slight movement of his head. Warned, Jack stood his ground, his stave countering the spear thrust. There was a splintering crack as the weapons met. Using all his force he twisted his stave round in a circular motion, as if unscrewing the lid on a jar. The guard's spear flew high into the air, the man gazing at it in disbelief. In the same movement Jack loosed one of his hands, aiming the end of his stave at the man's head. *Crack*! The guard fell to the ground and lay there stunned.

'Wow!' Jack exclaimed, 'Andy was right, it is easy if you watch their eyes.'

He swung round to see how Mercedes was getting on. She was bent over another of the guards who was bleeding copiously, blood pouring onto the stone staining it red.

'You've killed him,' he gasped.

'I don't think so!' said Mercedes sheathing her sword. 'Ran him through, though.'

They paused to watch the battle, controlled now by the warriors. The guards might be able to flourish their swords with bravado against a conventional enemy, but these were no conventional enemy. These were demons who kicked high and wide with their booted feet; feet so powerful that the guards fell winded and doubled-up in pain. As they staggered, they were felled by the merciless wooden staves, falling unconscious to the ground. Within minutes, those still left standing were desperately fleeing to reach the safety of their barracks, anything to escape this army of whirling dervishes. Despite their numbers, three guards to every warrior, they were no match for the speed and ferocity of the Riffs. They wielded their swords with such cunning, that their enemy never even saw them, until they felt the blade thrust and saw their blood pouring out on to the ground.

Ten minutes later, not one remained standing. They resembled no longer guards but a pile of inert logs, the courtyard and ramparts once again silent and empty.

Jack gazed about him. The courtyard remained silent, a peerless moon sailing above them in a starlit sky. The palace guards might now be unconscious, otherwise there was no sign that anything was wrong, the warriors immediately disappearing back into the shadows of the wall.

'Saleem, why isn't anyone coming out to see what's happening? Someone must have heard the noise. And what about the sentries at the gate?' he demanded.

Saleem waved the prisoners out into the fresh air of the courtyard.

'The people who live on this courtyard are mostly servants and helpers. They won't get involved until they know which side they're on,' he explained, his voice, for the first time ever, sounding sarcastic.

Suddenly, from behind them, a small door at the rear of the kitchens opened and nine boys ran out, carrying food and water.

Jack smiled at his football team. 'So that only leaves Saladin,' he said.

'We'll have to get rid of Saladin,' Mercedes said calmly. She wiped the blade of her sword on her trousers, sheathing it. 'Pops is otherwise engaged.'

'Excuse me, *oh worthless daughter of my worthless master*. Are you indeed the same person who pompously informed us, a minute ago, that her esteem-ed father had not told us to rescue the prisoners? Surely, you are now changing your coat, to suggest removing the tyrant from his throne?'

Mercedes glared at the camel. *Why you flea-bitten old carpet bag,* if Pops *had* got Prince Salah, he'd be back by now,' she retorted belligerently. 'He isn't,' she continued, 'so it's up to us. Sally, you stay here. If anythin' has happened to your father, you're the next ruler.'

'Not a chance. If I'm ruler then what I say goes and, anyhow, that makes me responsible for your safety.'

'She's right, Saleem. You should stay here.'

'NOPE!'

'*Sall-y!*'

'No, Merk, I'm going.'

'OK, I know when I'm beat,' the girl shrugged. 'So, Jack, how do I get the warriors out of the wall again?'

'OK! Say the words after me. *Manjilah vi Tubisaydah.*'

'*Manjilah vi Tubisaydah,*' repeated Mercedes.

Mercedes called the words into the air. For a moment everything was still, as if the entire universe was holdings its breath, then the shadows began to move again. The first ones stepped out of the wall dropping silently to the ground. Mercedes clapped her hands. Those still in the shadowy wall froze. The five warriors already liberated stalked towards her, their hands rising to their foreheads in the traditional gesture of a salaam.

'Bow,' she whispered to Saleem and Jack.

The warriors bowed low again – automatons, created without the ability to think or feel; simply react.

'Come on,' she called. 'And Bud, no cracks about my weight. You've got to carry the three of us to Saladin's quarters.'

The bells on Bud's harness rang out. 'You should have warned me, young master, when I was eating that I would be requiring the strength of thousands,' he said in a low whisper to Jack, who was shinning up his neck.

Jack laughed. 'Glad you haven't lost it, Bud. For a moment back there I thought you'd been injured you got so serious, and that'ud never do.' He turned to pull Mercedes up behind him. 'Saleem, you're going to have to hang on to Bud's tail and don't fall off.'

The bells on Bud's harness jingled again. 'Am I permitted to speak, young master.'

'What now, Bud?' Jack groaned.

'I was only going to say that never, in the whole of my history, have I had a prince hanging on to my tail. I am at a loss whether to feel insulted or honoured.'

'Bud, you crack me up,' laughed Saleem. 'Get on!'

Bud set off towards the bronze gate, his harness jingling softly in the still night air. There, as expected, they found the sentries lying senseless on the ground, having suffered the same silent fate as their companions.

'Go on, Bud – now it's Saladin's turn.'

Chapter Twenty

The Wall of Power

The high windows of Saladin's quarters showed light. 'That means he's awake,' Saleem whispered.

'Or fled,' suggested Mercedes, 'probably the latter. But why are we whisperin'? We all know he can't hear us.'

'Because there's something in that room a hell of a lot more powerful than Saladin, as Bud'll tell you,' retorted Jack, swinging round to glare at the girl.

'What?'

'A snake.'

'*Snake!* You never said anythin' about a snake.'

'Yes, I did, Mercedes, but I guess you weren't listening. It has some sort of power, like black magic. So speak only if you're forced to and, above all, keep your mind blank,' added Jack.

'Why?' the girl demanded.

'Because it takes over your mind. The only way I beat it was by building a wall in my head and, even then, I only just got out.'

Saleem shivered. 'We need Jacob. *We can't do this alone.*'

'We don't *have* Jacob, remember?' argued Jack. 'What we do have is the next best thing.' He pointed to the silent figures following the camel closely. 'Saleem, there's only us. We've got to do it.'

Saleem nodded his head miserably. 'I know.'

Bud passed easily through the studded doors, now guarded by a doubling of strength – a dozen guards outside in the courtyard, plus a dozen more, posted in front of the inner wooden doors, alert and ready for danger.

'We can handle them easy,' whispered Mercedes in Jack's ear, making to leap off the camel.

'No, Merk,' said Saleem. 'If there's any fighting, it has to be on the inside of the door where Saladin is.'

'But won't they come to his assistance?'

'Then, you'll get your fight, but not now, OK?'

Bud moved silently down the long corridor and, ignoring the men on guard, made for the doors.

'But can't the warriors be seen?' Jack said nervously.

'If I know Pops, he's left nothin' to chance,' Mercedes replied. 'See, the guards aren't suspicious at all.'

Jack glanced over his shoulder. To his astonishment there was nothing there, the corridor was empty. Startled, he peered more closely, identifying five phantom wisps of air passing unnoticed through the armed men.

Silently, the smooth molecules of the wooden door parted to let Bud, with his three riders, pass through. Saladin wasn't alone. By his side stood his faithful retainer, the man who acted as his armrest. He had opened one of the inlaid trunks and was examining its contents, his hands full of gold coins. Above them reared the snake, its coils curled around one of the carved boxes.

'Why is Saladin still here?' asked Saleem. 'Hasn't he got it yet that his number's up?'

'Obviously not, my Lord Saleem. See for yourself, he appears quite unperturbed. Do not forget the battle took place in the outer courtyard, well away from here, and none of the guards escaped to warn him.'

'But someone, surely ...' Saleem sounded confused.

'You, yourself, said that his people stay on the sidelines until they know which way the wind is blowing. Perhaps they are also reluctant to become the bearer of bad tidings. Whatever the real reason, he remains unaware of the attack.'

'So let's enlighten him,' shouted Mercedes, instantly forgetting Jack's advice about not speaking.

Saladin closed the lid of the trunk and stood up. His servant salaamed then, heaving it up on his back, disappeared through the small doorway that Saladin and his guests had used the previous night.

'But he's stealing our gold,' protested Saleem. 'He might be my uncle but he's no better than a common thief. We've got to stop him.'

Slowly, the snake's head moved, until it was looking right at them. It hissed loudly and bent its head low towards Saladin as if talking to him. Saladin called out, his eyes sweeping the room. Instinctively Jack ducked, convinced he'd been seen. He might know they were invisible but he still found it difficult to believe, especially with Saladin staring right at him.

The door flew open. A guard entered, his head almost touching the ground in respect. There was some conversation, with Saladin shouting and the guard touching his forelock, bowing constantly. The man swept his gaze round the room and shook his head.

'La,' he said and left the room, closing the door behind him.

Jack leant back and pulled at Saleem's jacket to get his attention. 'What was Saladin on about?' he whispered.

There was no reply. He swung round, alarmed to find Mercedes like a block of stone, her hands clamped over her ears, while Saleem appeared to be frozen, his eyes wide and staring.

Risking being heard, Jack pulled Mercedes' hand away from her ear.

'Mercedes build your wall,' he shouted and, reaching across her, shook Saleem. 'You too, Saleem, you've got to beat it. There's nothing in the room. Empty your mind, Saleem, and keep it empty. Just think of one nice thing – *the circus!*' he guessed desperately. 'Think of the high wire, swinging in the air, and empty space all around you.'

He knew he was spouting a load of drivel, but it didn't matter if it worked and he got through to his friends.

'*Empty Space!* Come on, Saleem; don't give up now! And you, Mercedes, think of fighting. *Use your sword. Go on. Use it!*'

The snake's eyes flickered, fixing themselves on Jack. At once the evil honed in on him, spiders pouring from every crevice of the room. He gazed in horror at their size; some as big as rats their legs a mile long, others with vicious faces and snapping jaws. The floor was covered with a thick carpet of brown bodies, closing in on the camel. They reached Jack's feet. Helplessly, he tried to kick them away, only to see them disappear up the leg of his jeans. Spellbound, he watched lumps appearing under the denim, moving about. They were in his trainers too, wriggling in and out of his toes; others high-wired it across the room, abseiling down into his hair and down the back of his neck. He shuddered, the hairs on his arms standing up in protest.

'*Go on, you extinct piece of garbage, give it your best shot,*' he shouted defiantly. '*I beat you once, I'll beat you again.*'

Suddenly, and where it came from Jack never knew, his mind flashed back to the movie he'd watched on Christmas Eve. It was supposed to be scary; instead it was funny, with thousands of glittering scarabs, rattling and clattering – like someone off-camera shaking a tin of beads – as they scuttled across the floor on their way to eat their next victim. He laughed out-loud. There was silence. The spiders had vanished!

'Saleem?'

'I'm okay, as long as I don't think.'

'You, Mercedes?'

'Nothing to it.'

Jack leaned over the camel's neck. 'Bud, you okay? *Jeez!* What's happening *now?*'

The snake's head, its forked tongue whipping in and out of the slit in its jaw, inched along the ground like a sniffer dog searching for drugs. Hissing loudly all the time, like a kettle about to boil, it slid slowly towards Saladin passing round him in a wide circle. White steam began to flow from its mouth. Expanding rapidly it spread upwards, rather like the wall Jack had tried to build in his head. Momentarily, the steam seemed to solidity into blocks of smooth white. Then, in a blink of an eye, it had vanished.

'Young master, I believe the snake is protecting Saladin with some sort of force.'

'That scum-bag. I mean, who in their right mind would want protect that mad man?'

'Shut-up, Mercedes! Go on, Bud.'

'I can feel it, but I cannot go further into the room. It is now too powerful.'

'That means we can't get to Saladin. *All this for nothing,*' Saleem cried out.

'Can you see the force, Bud?' Jack spoke in his normal voice. There wasn't any point whispering, the snake knew they were there.

'Yes, young master. To me it resembles a wall of thick air. It surrounds Saladin as if the snake's coils were all around him.'

'And this wall – whatever it is – does it go right up to the ceiling?'

'Not so far, young master, only as high as the snake's head.'

Jack stared at the snake, its head flicking menacingly from left to right in a constant search for intruders.

'Can you get over it?' asked Saleem eagerly.

'No, my Lord!'

'OK! OK!' muttered Jack. 'Now let's think. To get to Saladin we have to go over … ' He stopped in mid-sentence, looking up. 'Saleem, can you reach the chandelier in the centre of the room?' he whispered.

'From the balcony, no problem.'

'Yeah, right,' muttered Mercedes. 'Even under normal

circumstances that would be difficult, but how can you concentrate on climbin' and flyin', with thousands of spiders crawlin' everywhere.'

'I guess you don't like spiders,' said Jack innocently.

'Does anyone!' exclaimed the girl.

Jack hid his grin. 'Can you do it, Saleem? You held me up before and this'll be easy by comparison. Can I trust you to keep a hold?'

'Yes, Jack, no sweat.'

'OK! Get to the chandelier and swing it over to the balcony. I'll be waiting. You've got to swing us over that power wall; it's the only way to get to Saladin. Bud will tell us when we're clear, then drop me in the circle.'

'Young master, you cannot do this.'

'No, Jack, you can't,' said Saleem. 'It's far too dangerous. You can't face Saladin and the snake alone.'

'You're right, Sally, he can't. It's stupid. He's never even used a sword,' protested Mercedes indignantly. 'But I could.'

'*No way*, Mercedes! For starters, you can't hang from one hand. It's difficult enough for a boy, but a girl! *Now don't get mad,*' he added hastily, watching Mercedes' expression change. 'Besides, we need you here,' he admitted reluctantly. 'Don't you see, the moment we leave Bud and make for the stairs we become visible and the guards will be after us? Your job is to stop them. Anyway, it won't be Saladin and the snake. Saladin's gutless and if we get rid of the snake he'll give in – I know he will.'

'And if we don't?' asked Saleem.

'Then he wins and *I*, for one, am not going to let that happen.'

'OK! OK! OK! Let's go get'em before we have second thoughts,' called Saleem – and three hands flashed up in a high-five.

The two boys slid off the camel and sprinted for the stairs. Saleem reached the balcony first and, leaping on to its wide balustrade, untied the window chain nearest to him. Without hesitation, he launched himself into space, the chain spinning wildly and creaking under his weight. Controlling its spin, he started the chain swinging backwards and forwards, closing in on the next one. As it came within arm's reach, he grasped it firmly in his left hand setting it in motion also. Swinging hand over hand, he slowly moved from chain to chain, working his way across the ceiling space, drawing ever closer to the chandelier in the centre of the room.

Jack watched nervously, his eyes constantly drawn towards the snake, aware its gaze was fixed unblinking on him.

'OK, you monster, I know you don't like me.'

As he swung round to check on Saleem's progress across the roof space, a movement caught at the corner of his eye. Saladin had risen to his feet, a trickle of gold coins falling unnoticed from his fingers. He gazed upwards, staring in disbelief at the figure on the balcony. Jack wondered if he'd seen Saleem. But it was at him that Saladin was staring. Then he spoke, in that soft, slithery, unnerving voice that could well have belonged to the python.

'Mr Burnside, you are still at liberty. How very disappointing. Still, I assure you it will not be for long. See, I have raised the alarm and my guards will soon find you. Nevertheless, I must congratulate you on your audacity. Never before has anyone penetrated the security surrounding my private quarters.'

The door crashed open and guards burst in. For a second they didn't react, too startled at the appearance of a boy on the balcony in what had previously been an empty room. Yelling loudly, they made for the stairs and stopped dead. A lone warrior stood in front of them blocking the stairs. Its face obscured, its sword flashed through the air in a figure of eight, defying the soldiers to approach.

There came a burst of raucous laughter from the guards.

Then Mercedes whistled the four notes she had heard the Riffs use, during the fight in the courtyard. Instantly, five figures materialised beside her. Now six warriors blocked the stairs.

Shocked the guards gazed at one another. There was a murmur of voices as they hastily re-assessed the odds. *Six against twelve* – they charged.

'So this is your army, Mr Burnside – six men!' Saladin continued. 'Somewhat feeble, would you not say for a rescue attempt? I suggest you give in now, Mr Burnside, as defeat stares you in the face. Even if, by some miracle, you overpower my guards, you cannot proceed further into the room. The power of my guardian makes him *invincible*.' Saladin hissed the last word. 'And those you are come to rescue? Why, they are dead, Mr Burnside.

'I knew, Mr. Burnside,' Saladin lowered his voice to a mere whisper so that Jack had to strain forward to hear it. 'I knew, right from the moment I set eyes on you, and saw your refusal to pay me the respect I deserved, that you were trouble. I was right. Sadly, you have too little time left to learn that I am always right, for you will not live to see the light of day,' he hissed, his tone menacing. 'And since we are a country away from all countries, no one will ever know what has happened to you. That thought, Mr. Burnside, gives me *great* pleasure.'

He crossed to a couch and sat down, the snake encircling him. 'But indulge me, Mr Burnside, if indeed that is your name, why a mere boy should wish to enter my kingdom disguised as a footballer.'

'My name *is* Jack Burnside and I *am* a footballer,' Jack shouted. 'I came here to rescue my best mate, Saleem. Anyway, it's not me that's finished – *it's you. Look above you, Saladin.*'

Saladin's scream echoed round and round the room as he caught sight of Saleem swinging across the roof space. The boy grasped the iron bars linking the glittering icicles of the crystal chandelier and started it swinging. Grinning, he gave Jack a *thumbs-up* sign and, looping his legs over the bars, dropped headfirst down leaving both his arms flying free. Saladin, transfixed with horror, stared in disbelief

176

at the young prince. Backwards and forwards, like the pendulum of a clock, each time the curve of the swing increased to bring Saleem a little closer to the balcony edge where Jack waited.

'Come on, Jack, I won't let you drop.'

'I know,' called Jack and leapt for the outstretched hands and then, he too, was swinging free, high off the ground.

Instantly the evil surged towards him but now he knew how to beat it. He stared fixedly at the chain hanging against the wall, on the opposite side of the room, his mind totally blank and empty. Suddenly, he felt Saleem's hand begin to slacken and he slipped, realising the evil was attacking Saleem, probing for the weakest link.

'Saleem, *Saleem*, wake up,' he shouted. 'It's gunning for you 'cos it can't get me. Jeez, *Saleem! Come on! You can't let it beat you. Not now!*'

He reached up and grabbed Saleem's wrist, digging his nails into the palm of his friend's hand.

With a jolt, Saleem caught himself. 'Sorry, Jack, won't happen again.'

Jack felt the momentum increase, swinging them wider and wider. He loosed his grasp, holding himself on one arm, and felt for the sword at his side.

'Bud,' he shouted, hoping to be heard over the noise of the fighting below. 'Are we clear yet?'

Bud aimed his hind legs at one of the soldiers holding Mercedes. The man shouted and loosed his grasp. The girl twirled, plunging her sword through him.

'Yes, effendhi, you have cleared the wall of power.'

'One more, Saleem, and we're there!'

He pulled his sword from its scabbard, grasping it firmly. 'NOW!'

He hit the ground rolling, taking care to keep his sword arm free; then he was on his feet. Saladin, seeing the upraised sword, cowered back in terror but Jack wasn't interested in him. He was looking directly into the eyes of the snake rearing its head to strike, its tongue flicking, its gaze hypnotic.

'*Take that, you sleaze bag.*'

His sword bit deeply into the snake's neck. Jack raised it again. An involuntary muscle spasm sent the snake's coils whipping in his direction and its tail caught the back of his legs, toppling him to the ground. As he fell, he used the momentum to chop downwards into the leathery flesh. Immediately, the snake's hold slackened. He leapt quickly back onto his feet, only to see a coil come thrashing through the air and fasten round his sword arm. Swearing under his breath, Jack changed hands, grasping the sword tightly in his left. It wasn't as strong as his right but it would have to do.

He kept on attacking, awkwardly hacking again and again against the leathery skin. Each time his sword pierced the snake's flesh he regained his liberty, although the intervals were too brief to get within striking distance of the snake's head – a few seconds only – before another coil pinned him down.

Jack fought on determined not to be beaten, instinctively knowing that each time he wounded the reptile, he broke into its power source. If he could keep on, perhaps …

'Bud, help me,' he bellowed.

He swung his sword at the coil wrapped around his waist. Its razor-sharp edge sliced keenly through the thick epidermis, deep into the tender flesh below, severing nerve endings beneath the skin. Instantly, Jack felt the power source diminish, like a light bulb that dims and flickers before going out. He knew it wouldn't be for long, but it had to be enough for Bud to get through the wall.

He heard a roar and, chancing a glance over his shoulder, saw the camel fighting his way through the dense air of the wall; biting and kicking, screaming like a banshee. Next moment, he was there at Jack's side.

'Up, young master, up!' Bud ordered.

Jack needed no persuading. Grabbing the sword in his right hand again, he hacked furiously at a massive coil pinning his left arm. He felt a break in the power and dragged himself into the saddle.

If Mercedes and Saleem had looked now, they would have seen the snake fighting for its life, with Saladin cowering in his seat. But Mercedes was too busy to look, her sword flashing to stop a spear thrust, her warriors each engaging two men. And Saleem, intent on swinging his way back across the roof space to help, could not spare a glance, either.

Coil after coil dropped before Jack's sword yet always another barred his way, preventing him from reaching the snake's head. Even damaged, it was still capable of great harm, protecting itself with a barrage of coils while its evil magic healed its wounds. As the wounds closed over, there came a new surge of power. Once again, the snake reared its head over the boy, its power once more intact, poised to crush him and swallow him whole.

Jack saw the massive open mouth, its jaw unhinged, the inside blood red. The mouth gaped wider and wider enveloping him; its spitting tongue reached out to paralyse him, and then the crushing power of the evil burst out of the prison gates in his head, overwhelming him.

'Noooooooooooooo!' he yelled and, closing his eyes, thrust desperately upwards.

There was a screaming hiss and something heavy knocked him out of the saddle, crushing him to the ground. Then, there was silence.

Chapter Twenty One

The Ruler Returns

'Young *master, my Lord Burnside, infidel, effendhi, wake-up, wake-up, wake-up!*'

Jack slowly opened his eyes. *He was alive?* 'Am I alive?' he asked tentatively.

'You bet,' grinned Saleem.

'The snake?'

'Dead! Totally! Look for yourself.'

Jack sat up and gingerly rubbed his head, feeling very dizzy and sick. 'Have I a bump?'

'I'll say.'

'Thought so; it feels enormous.'

'It probably will be tomorrow but I don't think you'll care.'

'The guards?'

'No problem,' called Mercedes, calmly joining them.

'Saladin?' he asked, slowly getting to his feet.

'Disappeared froo that door,' said Saleem, pointing to the small doorway. 'Good riddance! It will save my farver the job of putting him on trial. And we saved most of the gold.' He pointed to a small trunk, upturned by the snake's convulsions, gold spilling out everywhere.

Bewildered Jack gazed at the carcass of the snake, its power gone; his sword thrust blindly upwards, piercing through its throat and into its brain.

'Did I do that?'

'Yes, young master, but almost at the cost of your life. Never again will I sneer at a christian …'

'You mean, never again will you wonder why conversations with christians end up going nowhere?'

'Yes, all right, *and that too.*'

Jack hobbled over to his camel and hugged his head. 'Bud, I wouldn't change you for the world. You go right on insulting me and anything else that takes your fancy. Without you, I'd be snake chow.'

'You can say that again,' grinned Mercedes. She stared round at the blood-spattered walls, the dead soldiers, and the huge carcass of the snake. 'Come on, let's get out 'a here. I tell you what, Sally, I don't see your father wantin' to move back here in a hurry.'

Saleem shuddered. 'No! I don't see any of us coming in here for a while; too many bad memories.'

'Bud, I know you're tired, but can you take us up one last time through the courtyard door?' said Jack, feeling somewhat fragile.

'Yes, young master, but where do you wish to go?'

'The kitchen, where else!' shouted the trio, climbing on his back.

The main gates to the palace stood wide open, the rest of Saladin's guards and supporters fleeing into the desert with their master, rather than meet up with unholy warriors, who fought like ten men. Several of the more able prisoners were collecting weapons and some had already armed themselves ready to fight, rather than be taken prisoner again.

Mercedes clapped her hands and her escort vanished back into the shadows of the wall, as Bud, tired but still game, walked slowly across the courtyard towards the kitchen.

* * *

'I tell you what, Pops is good.'

'You mean the warriors?' said Jack, chewing thoughtfully on a piece of meat.

Mercedes nodded.

'Is it over do you think?'

'You can't want another battle,' laughed Saleem. 'You bloodthirsty English!'

'No, I don't. I was just wondering.'

'But where is Pops?' demanded Mercedes.

As she spoke, the door to the kitchen opened and Jacob appeared.

'Ah, my daughter of infinite skill, but I am here. Where else would I be, may Jehovah be bless-ed. You are all safe? Ah, yes, I can see you are. Even that accurs-ed beast has succeeded in staying alive – which is a pity – for I begged the heavens to make sure he would be disembowelled in the fighting.'

Here we go again, grinned Jack, hearing Bud spit. *'Pfliipft!'* Peace had once more broken out.

'My farver?'

'I am here, my son, and safe, thanks to Jacob.'

A litter appeared, carried by four of the ghostly warriors, on which lay the frail figure of Prince Salah.

'Farver, you're hurt?'

'No! No! Weak only. Nothing that a little food and water won't cure if there is any left. I am too tired to think about ordering the cooks to get up.'

'Sir, there's plenty of food,' said Jack. 'Saladin had a feast prepared for after the match and it didn't all get eaten.'

He quickly found a plate and putting food on it carried it to the ruler, leaving Saleem to search the larders for milk. The prince filled a glass, perching himself on the floor beside his father.

'The kitchen seems an unlikely place to give my thanks to you all,' said the ruler in an exhausted voice.

'But Saladin escaped.'

'Yes, Jack Burnside, I know. That is not important. Of greater importance is the debt of gratitude that we owe you. If there is anything? Your head needs attention?'

'No, sir, it'll be fine. But you owe Saleem *and* Mercedes. Without them, we wouldn't have got through.'

'I agree wiv Jack, Farver. Merk here is great wiv a sword. I wouldn't like to face her, I know.'

'I confess to thinking it rather an unusual profession for a young lady.'

'My daughter has many unusual talents, my Lord Prince.'

'In this regard she is much like her father. Once again I am beholden to you, Jacob. And you, Jack Burnside, surely there is some reward I can give you?'

'Er ... no,' Jack started to shake his head. 'Oh ... well, *yes!* There is something – the servant boy, Yazim. Mendorun took him. Will you get him back as quickly as possible?'

'Does Jacob know about this?'

Jack nodded.

'Then it will be attended too, never fear.'

'Thank you, sir,' Jack said, knowing how frightened Yazim would be on his own in a strange place, and sad the boy had missed their match.

He glanced across at Jacob, standing straight and tall and powerful, his concern for the obvious frailty of the ruler keeping him close by his side. Then, in a blink of the eye, the image changed, and once again it was the familiar bent and twisted figure, his hands restlessly revolving round and round.

'Bud,' Jack whispered. 'That wasn't a trick of the light.'

'My accurs-ed master is a man of many disguises, effendhi. I keep telling you he is tricky,' came the gloomy response.

Jack took a deep breath. 'Jacob … you aren't really a merchant, are you?'

'But I am, my Lord Burnside, among many other things.'

'Huh!' snorted the camel in disgust.

'Surely, you cannot be surprised to hear that Saladin used spies to track down the men who had served Prince Sal-ah,' said Jacob. 'He knew he would never be safe until all his enemies were dead. I fled from town to town, finally settling in Mersham many miles away. I became a lowly merchant, of little interest to anyone; a moneylender, in order to glean information and a woodcarver, selling my wares, so I could move from market to market in safety.'

'But you're really a sorcerer – and a good one,' protested Jack. 'Surely you were safe?'

Jacob shook his head. 'It is the box that holds the power, not I. And, as you know, the box was lost to me.'

'And Bud?'

The camel, who had been feasting on hay, spat loudly, as if he had suffered a horrendous wrongdoing at the hands of his master. Immediately, Jacob's hands re-started their unending tirade around one another.

'Simply a wooden animal carved by me. And indeed greatly valued except for one thing – his cantankerous nature. In despair, I asked myself, perhaps I carved the wood against the grain? Maybe the wood had a knot in it? *Or both?* When, some years ago, I needed a loyal companion to serve my purpose, I bestowed on the statue the power of speech and life, and this is how he has repaid me. Indeed, the seven plagues of Egypt would be a far kinder punishment.'

'Huh! For all your threats, old man, you would be lost without me.'

'*So would I*, Bud, *so would I!* Can I keep him, Jacob? I kind 'a like having him around. Jeez!' Jack's hand flew to his mouth. 'I totally forgot. It's the seventh night and you promised I'd be home by dawn.'

'I told you not to listen to that leper's promises. Didn't I? Now look where it has got you!'

'Quiet beast or I will turn you into a sparrow and summon a hawk to feed upon you.' Jacob rounded on the camel. He turned back towards Jack, his hands raised in the air as if bestowing a blessing. 'Indeed, my Lord, if I am to keep my word, you must leave instantly. Indeed sooner than instantly.'

'First time ever,' came the muttered words from the corner.

'Thanks, Jack, you're a good mate,' said Saleem.

'I guess you're not coming back to training?'

Saleem shook his head. 'No, I'm needed here. You'll have to make do wiv the Nerd.'

'Yuck!' stuttered Jack in disgust. Then he grinned. 'Still, after what I've just gone through with Saladin, he'll be no problem.'

'Goodbye, Jack Burnside,' whispered Prince Salah, holding out his hand. 'I am deeply in your debt. I am only sad to have missed such a momentous match.'

'The match! *Oh, I forgot!*' Jack hit himself on the head with annoyance and let out a screech of pain. '*We won, Jacob!* You told me we'd lose but *we won*. You were wrong and I wish I'd had a bet on it.'

There was a chorus of laughter, even Jacob's eyes hinting at amusement.

'Come on then, Bud. Goodbye!'

He hugged his friends and, turning, mounted the camel unable to look back for the tears in his eyes. 'Take me home, Bud, I need my bed.'

'Yes, effendhi, but if you remember I always said that christians sleep too much.'

'Not quite right, Bud.'

'No, effendhi, but after a good rest, I, too, will be back to my normal self.'

'I look forward to it.'

Chapter Twenty Two

A Happy Christmas

'Infidel, we have a small problem.'

Hearing Bud's voice, Jack stirred, waking up out of a doze.

'What's that?' he questioned.

'The sun is rising behind us.'

'Jeez, Bud.' He swung round staring out to the east, noticing the horizon paler than the sky above them. 'Go faster can't you. If you get to the Alps, we'll be okay. It's bound to be cloudy over France.'

He felt their pace increase, the wind colder now whipping against his cheeks. Wishing he was back home and tucked up in a nice warm bed, he buried his face in Bud's neck urging him on, turning round anxiously to watch as the light began to gain on them.

'You just get there, Bud. You promised and Jacob promised, and I'm not falling out of the sky; not after all this.'

'That's easy for you to say, infidel. Perhaps, if you hadn't eaten so vastly during your holiday, I wouldn't now be having so much difficulty outrunning the dawn.'

Jack grinned. '*Holiday!* Some holiday, you grouchy old beast! Come on, we'll make it yet.'

The coastline of England was nearly upon them but so was the rising sun. Its rays lifted themselves over the horizon, catching the fleeing pair. Bud squealed and dived into the dark cloud base to escape. The flesh of the camel began to soften, turning to jelly beneath the anxious boy. He felt the camel once again lengthen its stride.

'You'd better not disappear, Bud. You owe me, you foul-smelling, unreliable animal. *You're not going to turn into a jelly, not now!*'

He felt himself falling. 'NO!' he shouted.

His road! His house!

He heard himself shout again and then he hit something very hard.

He sat up gingerly, feeling the pain in his head where he had banged it on his bedroom floor. *Jeez!* He was going to have such a bruise tomorrow, but he was home. They had done it, they had actually done it. He gazed down at the floor. *Thank goodness, Bud was okay.* He picked up the statuette and hugged it tightly, before replacing it on the windowsill.

'Thanks, Bud, now I've got to sleep.'

It was his sister shouting that eventually woke him. He leapt out of bed, gazing wildly about him unsure of where he was. Then he remembered. He stared down at the mess on his floor, his rucksack lying in the middle of a heap of clothes. *And Bud?* Panicking, he looked across at the windowsill. *Phew!* He was there, exactly as he'd left him, the supercilious look firmly in place.

Jack picked up the camel feeling the wood warm in his hands. 'Wow, Bud, you've got a burnt tail! No wonder you squealed,' he whispered. 'What a Christmas.' He patted the camel. 'See you tonight.'

The scent of cooking wafting up from the kitchen reminded him that it was Christmas Day and he was starving. Showering quickly, he ran downstairs and glanced in through the open living room door. The dark green fir tree twinkled at him – a pile of mouth-watering, brightly coloured boxes beneath its gaily-decorated branches.

He pushed open the kitchen door.

'Happy Christmas, Mum; Happy Christmas, Luce.' he said, giving them both a hug. 'When can we open our presents?'

'When Grandma and Auntie Maeve get here. Hurry up and have your breakfast; it's almost lunchtime and they'll be here in a minute.'

The doorbell rang.

'Oh no! They're early and I haven't finished doing the vegetables. Be an angel, Jack, and get the door – *but take your time.* And *please* be nice to them.'

'OK, Mum, no sweat.'

Jack walked as slowly as possible across the hall. *Well,* he told himself, *if the relatives get too frightful, I'll just get Bud to whisk me off somewhere extra dangerous.*

And with a broad smile, he opened the front door.